The Greatest Breakthrough since Lunchtime

COLIN DOUGLAS (a pseudonym) was born in 1945, graduated in medicine some years ago, and since then has worked in a number of jobs at home and abroad, at sea and on land.

The Houseman's Tale, his first novel, won the John Rowan Wilson Award, presented annually for wit, style and lucidity in treating medical subjects. *The Greatest Breakthrough since Lunchtime* was his second book and his latest is *Bleeders Come First,* the sequel to *The Houseman's Tale* and *The Greatest Breakthrough since Lunchtime.*

D1389909

Available in Fontana by the same author

Bleeders Come First
The Houseman's Tale

The Greatest Breakthrough since Lunchtime

Colin Douglas

Fontana/Collins

First published in 1977
by Canongate Publishing Ltd
First issued in Fontana Books 1978
Second Impression May 1980

Made and printed in Great Britain by
William Collins Sons & Co Ltd, Glasgow

Author's Note

In real hospitals, there are strict rules
governing experimentation upon patients;
in fictional hospitals, of course, these rules
may be partially or completely ignored.

ONE

'When that breast comes up, get a bit for me, please.'

The girl sitting next to Campbell in the observation gallery of the operating theatre yawned and stretched and then got up. She pushed a little bottle along the bench towards him.

'What?'

'The breast. The breast third on the list. I want a bit.'

'I see.'

She was looking at Campbell as if he had clearly not seen. 'She's the only one this week under eighty. And we want cycling women.'

'Cycling?'

'Having menstrual cycles. They've got to be or it's no good.'

'What isn't?'

'The research.'

'Oh.'

She was speaking as though Campbell, by his perverse ignorance, were deliberately making a nuisance of himself and delaying her departure. 'We're doing something that needs fresh breast from cycling women. It changes.'

'What does?'

'The epithelium. You can tell what stage of the cycle it's at.'

'Couldn't you just ask them?'

She threw him a look of cold impatient disdain. Campbell opted to play a little harder. 'I suppose you couldn't really because they're asleep.'

'What?' She almost shrieked.

'Only joking,' said Campbell mildly.

'What do you mean?'

'Sorry. A joke. I said you could have just asked her. But

you can't because she's anaesthetised.'

'I see,' she said quickly, with a millisecond smile and half a giggle. 'Basically it's a histochemical method. We're looking at diphospho-dephospho-transphosphorylase. It might have something to do with cancer.'

'Well, have fun.'

Again she stiffened with impatience and importance, jabbing a finger at the bottle on the bench. 'We won't have anything if you forget about that specimen.'

Her own breasts were large and despite the conical, reined-in effect of a rather old-fashioned bra, did things for her white coat.

'Will I get my name on the publication if I remember?'

She turned and stood over him, menacing him with two heavy cones possibly packed solid with diphospho-dephospho-transphosphorylase. She snapped, 'You don't seem to take research very seriously,' then turned and walked away, pausing at the door to say, 'The breast, third on the list. If you don't mind.'

Her second last remark was scarcely fair: Campbell who had been in research only since nine that morning, had had little time to acquire views of any sort. His own research, about which he had not as yet, it was true, learned much, seemed sterner stuff. At least it was in the large intestine and therefore the concern of all the human race, not just half of it. He tried to think of other reasons why it might be better.

'Don't worry about her. She sometimes goes like that. Phases of the moon more than likely.' The man remaining at the other end of the bench was lean and nasal. There was a bottle beside him too.

'It might be that phospho stuff, making them all go mad.'

'Might be. My wife's the same.' The words marked him as an Australian. 'Only with her it's ovulation. She goes wild. Cleans everything and paints all the cupboards. Gets randy as a bush-ranger's bitch too. I really have to watch my step. We're Catholics, see.'

'You doing research?'

He looked puzzled. 'In that?'

'No. Research. Here.' Campbell pointed at the little bottle.

'Oh, that. My job? Yeah, I'm in the muscle zinc programme.'

'Looking for bits of muscle?'

'Yeah. Anything that's going. Regardless of age, sex, colour or creed. But there hasn't been anything this morning. Yet.'

'None at all? Not even abdominal stuff?'

'It's no good. We need regular half-inch cubes.' It sounded like a recipe. 'There's not much on the abdomen that size. Not over here anyway.' Campbell had a vision of surfriders and monstrous tanned tennis girls queueing to donate their half-inch cubes to science. 'In fact to tell you the truth we've only had a couple of really good bits in the last month. And one was at half past three on a Friday, for Christ's sake.'

'D'you like research?'

'It's okay. As research goes.' He suddenly stuck out his hand. 'McGavigan.'

Campbell shook the proffered hand. 'David Campbell.'

'Hi, Dave. I'm Ainslie McGavigan.'

The combination of the absurdity of the Australian's name and the wanton abbreviation of his own caused Campbell to flinch inwardly. Like a jaded chess player starting a duty match he pushed out with 'How long have you been over here?' and switched off.

McGavigan proved an undemanding conversationalist. Campbell sat through the journey, the housing problem, the British climate, the Scottish public and the way it spoke English, with no particular regrets about having triggered it all off. It was as interesting as the surgery below. He wondered if the man would talk spontaneously about the mysteries of life in research or if some pumping would be necessary. And the wife thing might be interesting too if he got back to it. He did not. He covered relative prices of a variety of services, foods and household goods, then standards of politeness among public employees and then moved on to the relative cost and quality of Australian and British wine, though he seemed to be construing the latter term to include French, Italian and, for all Campbell knew, Yugoslavian products.

Under the windows of the viewing gallery the operating theatre staff went through the slow rituals of cleaning and robing, cutting and stitching, passing silvery instruments across the field of mystical green. The indeterminate figures, also in green, mumbled inaudibly behind their masks and the glass of the observation gallery. It was all very soothing. The Australian droned on about a man he had met in a pub and Campbell sensed himself in an equilibrium, a temporary calm at the centre of several slowly revolving currents of absurdity, and was briefly and precariously happy because, without physical or intellectual effort he was, in a sense, working. He was waiting for a piece of someone's large bowel, and until he got it he could not begin his research.

The figures below began to disrobe again. The patient was unveiled and mopped and the chest strapped over and over with firm swathes of sticking plaster. A technician carried something out of the theatre in a bucket. McGavigan interrupted himself. 'Jeeze, you forgot her bit of tit. She'll kill you.'

'Hell.'

'You said you would.'

The girl had been unpleasant enough just asking him. Campbell wondered what she would be like when he told her he had forgotten. The possibility that she might be fooled by a piece of someone's large bowel or a regular half-inch cube of something else occurred to him but was quickly dismissed. Honesty was beginning to look like the only policy. Caveats along the lines of 'not really my job' were all subsumed in the general admission of liability implied in his tacit agreement to do it. The bottle with its clear pool of preservative sat accusingly at his side.

'Who is she anyway?'

'Jocasta somebody. Smith, I think.'

'Jocasta?'

'Calls herself Jo.' If she didn't you would, thought Campbell. 'Works in some big breast study they've got here.'

'Well, she's got the figure for it.'

'Yeah. Rockyboobs. Hearts of stone and a bosom to match. What are you after?'

'What?'

McGavigan pointed to Campbell's little bottle.

'Oh. Gut.'

'Anything in particular?'

'Large bowel.'

'You sure you're in the right theatre? There's nothing like

that on the list that I saw.'

'I think I am. A diverticulitis for colostomy. He was on the list I read.' In the circumstances there might be something to be said for leaving an apology to be passed on to Dr Jocasta Whoever by McGavigan, and going down to check with the surgeons on what had happened to the man who by his unwitting generosity had been about to launch Campbell into a career in medical research.

'She'd have killed you,' said McGavigan. 'Now she'll just kill me instead.'

'Thanks.'

It was odd to be back. Campbell had trained at the Institute and worked there as a houseman for seven months of his pre-registration year before falling victim to hepatitis in a hospital outbreak in which one of his fellow housemen had died. After three months' convalescence and a spell in a peripheral hospital as a house surgeon he had returned to a research post attached to his old medical unit. Little at the Institute had changed. The sense of oddness Campbell experienced amounted only to a feeling akin to that of going back to school in the middle of term, for private reasons vanishingly unimportant in relation to the massive continuing ordinariness of institutional life. The smell on the surgical corridor was exactly as it had been eight months previously.

Downstairs Campbell found the entrance to the theatre and went into a rest room where two nurses, a callow youth presumed to be the houseman, and a large heavy surgeon were sitting around chatting. The large man, whom Campbell recognised as the surgeon who had done most of the cases on the list, still had his mask on.

'Excuse me, I wonder if you could tell me what's happening about one of the cases on your list.' On grounds of his relative youth the large man did not merit even a tentative 'sir'. 'There was a diverticulitis for colostomy. I'm attached to the faecal vitamin pilot study and wondered if I might have some of the mucosa. Not a lot. I don't think it matters where it's from. Anywhere in the colon.'

'God, lad,' said the surgeon. 'I never expected to see you in the kebab squad.'

'Hadden!'

'For it is he,' said Hadden, taking his mask off and grinning. 'Where have you been for the last however long it is?'

'Being ill. Then doing locums.'

'Of course. Being yellow.'

'Being yellow and ill, then doing locums in peripheral surgical units to register.'

'I must hear your memoirs sometime. See you in the pub at five.'

'Great. What about the colon?'

Hadden rolled his eyes piously and pointed heavenwards. 'It came to a full stop.'

With the morning's work either completed or rendered impossible, depending on which way you looked at it, and the time at only about a quarter past eleven, Campbell found himself thinking around for things to do before lunch. He had already read his *Guardian*, which had seen him through the longish coffee break between his brief introductory session with Dr Fyvie and his sojourn in the observation gallery. It occurred to him that he might return to his desk in the research fellows' room via the hospital shop, picking up a *Telegraph* on the way. He started out in that direction and on his way met a nurse he had once worked with. They talked for a little while and he found himself explaining what he was now doing with a deliberate vagueness arising from his own feeling that he had not really found out yet.

She was a friendly, not unattractive girl whom Campbell would probably have asked out the previous year but for reservations about her accent. She told him about a forthcoming party in the flat she shared with five other nurses. He thanked her and scribbled the address and date on a piece of paper on which he had also noted down the main points of Dr Fyvie's guidance on his project.

When he got to the shop the idea of reading the *Telegraph* before lunch seemed more reprehensible than it had done at first. He bought some Polo mints instead. Talking to the nurse about his research project had revived his interest in it a little. He took out his piece of paper again and read it as he walked along the corridor back to his room. In block capitals at the

top he had written 'FAECAL VITAMIN PILOT STUDY : PHASE TWO' followed by the names of the various members of staff in Dr Fyvie's unit and elsewhere whose expertise, in her phrase, would be available to him. She had suggested a basic method for the colonic mucosa experiment and told him about the lab where it might be done. He should 'just play around with it for a day or two' and 'read himself into the field' over the first week. She would be available for further advice at any time, by appointment with her secretary, and looked forward to hearing from him on the subject at the end of the first fortnight; by which time he should have reviewed the relevant literature and summarised it with his own gathered thoughts on the matter on a few sides of foolscap, preferably typed, and not, please not, more than about five thousand words. Such had been Campbell's introduction to the research aspects of his brave new job.

His desk in the research fellows' room was very much the new boy's : it stood in the corner farthest from the door, under a draughty window, and but for the *Guardian* was as naked as the day it had emerged from the furniture van. The five other desks in the room were variously covered with tidy and untidy collages of index cards, photocopied references, scrawled manuscripts, green and white striped computer print-out paper, microscope slides, typed or handwritten tables of results, telephones, tape-recorders and little bottles of a type with which Campbell had already become familiar. The only other person in the room was a round-faced African of about his own age, sitting at another corner desk reading the *Financial Times*.

Campbell sat down momentarily at his desk. It was too late in the morning to go across to the university library and start reading his way into his subject. It was still too early to go for lunch. He decided to jot down in more detail a record of his conversation with Dr Fyvie, which he now saw as the foundation stone of his career in research. He began to look in the drawers of his desk for some paper. There was none. The drawers were all empty, but for a totally inexplicable brown shoelace in the top right-hand one. Once more he felt very new at the game.

A glance at the other desks told him that one of the things

required for a career in research was a plentiful supply of paper, so rather than settle for the temporary and untidy solution of borrowing some from the African he determined to acquire a whole packet, and set out along the corridor to the unit secretary's room. It was empty and all the cupboards were locked.

When he got back to the research fellows' room the African was on the phone. '. . . never was very keen on those things and today might be the day for getting rid of them. See what happens to them this afternoon, howevah, and ring me back if anything of interest takes place. Otherwise just sell 'em. . . . Okay . . . okay. Really? Well in that case hang on to them and see. . . . No, it's no trouble. Better safe than sorry. I'll either be on this extension or at home all afternoon. Thank you again. Good day.' He put the phone down, folded his *Financial Times* and picked up the *Scotsman*.

Campbell asked if he might borrow some paper. The African handed him the *Financial Times* and said, 'May I borrow your *Guardian* this afternoon? Fair exchange?'

'Certainly. Thanks. But I meant foolscap actually.'

'Let me see.' He riffled through a heap on his desk. 'No joy. May I suggest you borrow from her.' He indicated the empty desk in front. 'It seems that we have not as yet actually met. Roddy Abavana.'

'David Campbell.'

'I see we both have at least one good Scottish name. The Roderick is the missionary influence.'

'Really?'

'You Scottish presbyterians. My country owes a great deal to the missionary influence. Anyway, I must not be keeping you from your work.' He returned to the financial pages of the *Scotsman*.

It was only a quarter to twelve. Campbell laid the notes from Dr Fyvie's introduction on his desk and headed up a page of borrowed foolscap 'FAECAL VITAMIN PILOT STUDY : PHASE TWO'. Then he remembered that his new post also carried clinical responsibilities.

In turning to his clinical duties Campbell felt that he might find himself once more on firmer ground. In a simple unreflective way he enjoyed looking after patients: that was what he had trained for. The beds which Dr Fyvie had entrusted to his care were in the wards where he had served his time as a house physician, less than a year before. His return was a kind of promotion: he was to look after Dr Fyvie's female in-patients, supervising the work of the house physician and assessing each new patient and planning their management. He would do rounds himself to check on progress and therapy and accompany the great lady on her own Friday ward rounds.

The full implications of his promotion did not strike him until he was sitting at the desk in the duty room, reading the case notes. When last thus seated, he had been right at the bottom of the medical heap, the hapless functionary whose task it was to obey all orders and look after all patients. The sense of liberation amounted to little more than the knowledge that whoever came through the door next would probably not be looking for him, but that, compared to the houseman's lot, was a great advance. That feeling, together with the absence from his pocket of the hateful and burdensome bleep by which anyone capable of using a phone could summon him at any time of the day or night, made his new status well worth while.

He read the case notes with a growing sense of his power and importance. Most of the writing would now be done by someone else. Dr Fyvie, fairly characteristically, had told him nothing about the houseman on the ward, but as he sat, reading the admissions and the progress notes, certain impressions emerged from good clear handwriting and some nice firm phrases ('a wee thin old lady') which were a welcome alternative to the flaccid jargon comprising the bulk of medical communication. Progress notes were regular and lucid. The lab forms were all firmly stuck on the appropriate pages of the folder. (He remembered one of his own lower moments as a houseman, when the senior registrar in his surgical unit had shaken a case-folder by the spine and it had taken him ten minutes to sort out the resulting heap on the floor.) On the forms the houseman's signature was also agreeably legible: J. Moray.

J. Moray would now be carrying the bleep which had once

ruled Campbell's own life. He picked up the phone and asked the exchange to bleep Dr Moray, put it down and waited.

The phone did not immediately ring in answer: housemen were getting slack. Campbell waited in the sunlit room. It had been painted since his tenure, with two orange and two white walls in place of the oppressive uniform institutional pale blue of his time, and was now almost pleasant. A blackbird was singing outside. He was beginning to feel hungry. He looked at his watch.

A girl came in with a big syringe full of blood and a lot of laboratory specimen tubes: she stood them in a row on the bench and filled them then put the plastic tops on. She was tall, with medium length brown hair. From the absence of the outward and visible signs of housemanship – bleep, tendon hammer, notebook and the like – and the minor but positive finding that her white coat was not quite freshly laundered, Campbell took it that she was a senior student attached to the ward for training. She should at least know the whereabouts of the doctor whose bloods she was doing.

Campbell was about to ask her but was interrupted by the sound of a bleep going off. She reached into her pocket and silenced it, then said, 'Sorry, I'll really have to answer that. It's the third time they've bleeped me.' She picked up the phone and said, 'Dr Moray on two one three nine.' There was a short pause then she smiled and said, 'Okay, I'm on it.'

'Sorry,' said Campbell. 'I was bleeping you but I didn't know it was you.'

'It's all right.'

'I'm Dr Campbell. Dr Fyvie asked me to take over her female beds from Dr Dempster. Can we go round?'

She sat down on a chair opposite, putting her elbow on the desk and cupping her chin in her hand. She looked at him and said, 'You're the fifth this morning.'

'Sorry. I could come back in the afternoon. Or just go round on my own. I've been reading the case notes.'

'No, I'm just moaning. You know what it's like.'

'Yes, I worked here.'

'So I've heard. And I've seen some of your case notes.'

Campbell was fairly sure that his case notes reflected a less creditable approach to medicine than hers. They were illegible because that was the way he wrote and he was usually tired when he did his progress notes, and sometimes because a certain calculated obscurity might give him the benefit of the doubt with the registrars.

'Let's do it now,' she said. 'Before lunch.'

When she picked up the case notes Campbell noticed for the first time that she had a plain, rather narrow gold band on the third finger of her left hand. They went into the ward together.

As in the days of yore, Dr Fyvie's patients were distinguished by large pink stars on their temperature charts, together with the legend 'Dr Rosamund Fyvie' in large black capitals to eliminate doubt completely. The patient's name, in smaller and fainter writing, came much farther down the chart.

The 'wee thin old lady' was the first thus labelled patient they came to in the ward. In addition, her temperature chart carried a large notice saying 'Fasting' in red and a smaller card with 'FVPS' in blue.

'What's "FVPS"?'

'Faecal Vitamin Pilot Study,' said Dr Moray.

'Oh . . . What's wrong with her?'

'Nothing to do with vitamins. A stroke. Left sided. She's sweet. Lived down the Canongate. Got a dozen grandsons, mostly coalmen. They come and visit her at funny times. Sister's not keen but she lets them.'

Campbell found himself glad to be back on the wards. Dr Moray moved closer to the patient, who looked like a clean and friendly witch. When she was very close the witch, with a start, noticed her.

'Oh, it's you, hen. Ah'm awfy hungry.'

'Yes, it's for a wee test this afternoon.'

'But I've had nothing at all since last night.'

'Go on. You had your breakfast.'

'Only a wee piece of toast and some porridge I could hardly chew.'

'You'll get something special when you come back from the test. I'll make sure.'

'Thanks, hen.'

Dr Moray raised her voice. 'Mrs Innes, I've brought a new doctor to see you.'

'Anither?'

'Yes. He'll be looking after you instead of Dr Dempster.'

'Dr who?'

'The doctor who was looking after you before. This one's Dr Campbell.'

'Hello, Mrs Innes.'

'Hello, son.'

'What age are you, Mrs Innes?'

'Ninety I think. Something like that.'

'She's eighty-four,' said Dr Moray. 'She lies about her age.' The patient clutched Campbell's hand. 'Dinnae listen tae her, son. She's just a wee lassie. I'm ninety-six and I'm going to live to my telegram.'

'How long's she been here?'

'Longer than I have. I got her in the handover from the last houseman. He said, "Don't worry about her, she just lives here." '

'So what's she fasting for?'

'A PVPP.'

'What on earth for?'

'To validate a new method for upper gut bacterial estimation. One of Bill Dempster's things.'

'What's wrong with her upper gut bacteriology?'

'Nothing really. They're comparing the methods.'

'How come Bill got interested?'

'She's got a small duodenal diverticulum.'

'Any symptoms? Pain? Sickness? Diarrhoea?'

'No.'

'How the hell did they find out?'

'Bill read a series somewhere, saying that twenty-three per cent of two thousand barium meals in symptomless females over eight showed diverticula. So she had a barium. Her bad luck it was abnormal.'

'Tough. How's her stroke coming on?'

'All right. But no one's very interested in that.'

'Ah'm fine,' said the patient, in her high, grating voice.

'Let me see,' said Campbell. 'Grip my hands. Squeeze my fingers. Pull me towards you.'

'I would too, if I was younger.'

Dr Moray smiled. 'Don't worry. She fancied Bill too. Anything in trousers. Don't you, Mrs Innes?'

'Can she walk?'

'She walks not too badly.' Dr Moray raised her voice. 'Get up and let Dr Campbell see you walk.'

'Whit?' said the patient.

Dr Moray raised her voice further. 'Dr Campbell wants to see you walk.'

'What are you saying?' said the patient.

Dr Moray stooped over her and shouted in her ear, 'This new doctor wants to see you walk,' then stood up quite close to Campbell. She was a little red in the face, and grinning. She laughed and remarked to Campbell, 'Sometimes she's a little deaf.'

'I'm quite comfortable where I am,' said the patient, 'and I'm ninety-six and I haven't had any breakfast.'

'Okay,' said Campbell. 'Have you seen her walk recently?'

'Yes. This morning.'

The patient had drawn the blankets round herself and was staring fixedly straight ahead to indicate that the interview was at an end.

'Who's next?' said Campbell.

'This way,' said Dr Moray. Their elbows touched briefly as they walked up the ward.

Dr Fyvie's next patient was a middle-aged woman who was deeply jaundiced, a sight that jolted Campbell a little from his professional objectivity. He asked the house physician about her before they got within hearing range. She came up close to him, so close he could smell her hair, a clean vaguely medicated-shampoo smell, and talked quietly.

'Mrs Herron. Forty-five. She's my real problem in here just now. Primary biliary cirrhosis. And she used to be a physiotherapist here in the Institute. I think she's got a fair idea what's going on. She's got a husband and a couple of really nice kids.' She paused and looked very seriously into Campbell's eyes. 'I think they're beginning to think mum's not going to come home.'

'They could be right. How's Dr Fyvie playing it?'

'Cheerfully. You know what she's like. A bit jolly-hockey-sticks and how-are-we-today?'

'I can imagine. There's no doubt about the diagnosis?'

'Not much. They've looked for everything you can have with it and she's got most things. Smooth muscle antibodies, immunoglobulins, ESR, negative barium everywhere except for the oesophageal varices. Liver scan fits too. And she's had a couple of biopsies.'

'Conclusive biopsies?'

'Pretty well. Dr Dempster was planning to do another last week but he called it off. There were problems about bleeding. Her pro. time is sky high.'

'Difficult. What's she on?'

'Diet. Vitamin K injections. Immuran. Good response to Immuran at first. Not so much now.'

The patient had put down her book and was politely waiting for the doctors to finish their conversation about her. She was haggard and yellow, with brownish circles under her eyes and abdominal swelling that was obvious even under the bedclothes. Her arms were thin and discoloured by the bruises of many samplings of blood. Campbell talked to her and examined her and when he had finished realised why she seemed to the house physician the most difficult problem on the ward. As he replaced the bedclothes the patient spoke.

'I didn't catch your name, doctor.'

'Oh. Sorry. Campbell. Dr Campbell. . . . I'm Dr Fyvie's . . . I'm in Dr Fyvie's team.' To explain his exact clinical status, as honorary senior house officer to Dr Fyvie by virtue of his junior research fellowship, would have been tedious or pedantic or both. The absurdly sporting overtones of his explanation were an acceptable price to pay for brevity. She smiled understandingly. 'There are so many of you around. Will you be working here for some time?'

'I should think so,' said Campbell. 'At least a year.'

She looked at him thoughtfully. 'I've seen so many doctors. And they seem to come and go so confusingly.' It sounded as if she wanted to talk for longer. Campbell sat on the edge of her bed, a practice resented by nurses but appreciated by most patients. It was a way of saying 'I'm not hurrying away' which Campbell had picked up as a houseman from Bertram, the registrar. He waited for her to say something else.

'Doctors come and go,' she said quietly, 'but I seem to stay. Well, not continuously. But I've spent more time in here than out in the last six months.'

Campbell could see that she had been pretty once: though lean and jaundiced, her features were fine and still not unpleasing. Her eyes were large and calm and enquiring.

'So I've heard,' said Campbell.

'I keep wanting to go home, and if I pester them a bit they let me . . . then I don't feel as well as I thought I would and have to come back.' And she had been a physiotherapist who had worked and probably trained at the Institute some twenty-five years ago. Campbell tried to imagine her as a sleek, bouncy girl, wearing whatever uniform they wore in the late forties, and working on the wards. Physios were oftener deb than pleb, and probably more so then: her accent fitted in with that. On the wards she would have seen patients getting thinner and yellower, and would know what happened to most of them.

'How d'you feel right now?'

She smiled. 'Well enough to want to go home but not well enough to go. And anyway there are the tests. "A few tests," Dr Fyvie said.' She smiled again. 'She always says that: "Just a few more tests."'

'It's not a very straightforward jaundice,' said Campbell lamely. 'Dr Moray's been telling me about you.'

'Oh, I'm not ungrateful. Everybody's kind. And if something's going to hurt it's usually explained beforehand. . . . I sort of trust the place as much as I trust the people. I trained here.'

'Oh?'

'Physiotherapy. Worked here for a while too. And came back after the children.'

'What was that like?'

'A bit strange. While I was having a family, physiotherapy was sort of demilitarised. I got teased for being a bit of a drill-sergeant. It's nice though, watching the girls now. Lots of it hasn't changed.'

Campbell smiled and made to get up. She put out a hand towards him and said, 'Dr Campbell, how long do you think I'll . . . be in this time?'

He sat down again. 'Depends on how you feel. And on what Dr Fyvie thinks. From what you say it sounds as if we

shouldn't rush things. I'm going off to read all about you.'
He indicated the case folder, two inches thick, in the house
physician's bundle.

'Thank you, Dr Campbell.'

Campbell felt that he had been given permission to get up
and go away, and did so. The two doctors left her bed.

'Who's next?'

The next patient, a girl of about fifteen, was, like the first
patient on the round, fasting. Dr Moray explained without
comment that Dr Dempster's new method involved expensive
radioactive material which had to be used shortly after de-
livery. The patient had had her PVPP the previous day and
an appointment with Dr Dempster had been arranged for
that afternoon.

'Does he think there's anything wrong with her upper
gut?'

'No. Her barium and endoscopy were both normal. He wants
normal controls too.'

'What's she in for?'

Dr Moray smiled. 'Vague abdominal pain.'

Campbell addressed the patient. 'How's the pain now?'

Dr Moray turned to him and said quietly, 'She's from St
Cuthbert's Hospital, Crewe Toll.'

'Oh.' Now that his colleague had mentioned where the
patient had come from, Campbell noticed certain things
about her: the girl had a small round head, a protruding
tongue, ears like teacup handles and funny little red eyes.

'Grooogh.' She made a moist gargling sound and drooled
quite a bit.

'I see,' said Campbell. 'Any problems?'

'Not really,' said Dr Moray.

The patient seized her arm delightedly, jabbering 'Nice
doctor nice doctor', and was beginning to chew her sleeve. Dr
Moray shook her off gently and put an arm round her shoulders for a moment.

They walked up the ward a little and stopped.

'How did she get in here?'

'There was definitely something wrong with her when she
came in. Not sure what it was, but it's gone away. She's a

happy kid. The nurses all pet her like mad. They're very fond of her.'

'Has Dr Fyvie got any views on when she might be getting back to Crewe Toll? She must miss the nuns.'

'Dr Dempster might have views.'

'Oh. I see. Who's next?'

'That's it.'

'Only three?'

'Sometimes you'll have four. It's the new quota system. Rosamund was really pushing her luck in spring and early summer. She had sixteen in once. Dr Creech and Dr Kyle got together and worked out the quota system. Then when Dr Young was appointed a consultant here they all had to take another cut.'

'Well, it's nice to hear that Creech and Kyle agreed about something.'

'Yes . . . What did you think of Mrs Herron?'

'Mmm. She's got the lot. Palms, nails, naevi, bruising, finger clubbing. And a tremendous liver. A real beginner's special. Jumps out on to your hand. You could feel it from the end of the bed.'

'That's how Rosamund sees her. An invaluable teaching case. Mrs Herron's very good about it all. She told me once when I was taking blood from her that fifty-three people had felt her liver since she came in.'

They walked towards the door. At the top of the ward, Sister stood behind her lunch trolley. Her starched, frilled cap, an enormous spoon held like a sceptre, and the little row of three nurses standing on each side of her gave the appearance of royalty depicted by Tenniel for Lewis Carroll. She smiled primly and said, 'Good morning, Dr Campbell. It's actually good afternoon by two minutes but I'll overlook that. It's a pleasure to have you back on the ward after such a long absence. So long that you seem to have forgotten that the patients' lunches on this ward begin at twelve o'clock sharp.'

When they had passed Sister's lunchtime levée and were walking towards the doctors' room, Dr Campbell and Dr Moray found themselves looking at each other and laughing.

'Thanks, Dr Moray. You seem. . . .'

'Jean.'

'Thanks, Jean. You seem to have things under control.'

'Do I? That's nice. Mrs Herron's the only difficult one of that lot.'

'Medically? Socially?'

'Medically. . . .' Campbell resolved to go away and read a great deal about primary biliary cirrhosis that afternoon. '. . . and socially as well.'

'Who knows what?'

'That's the problem.'

They went back to the doctors' room and sat down. The place had changed in other ways than simply redecoration: it was much tidier. There were no heaps of unfiled lab reports and no rows of untested unmentionable specimens. The working surfaces were all empty and clean and the equipment stowed neatly, the case notes were all filed away except Rosamund's three, which lay on the desk between them. There was a new wooden rack for holding the bundles of blank lab forms and a clever moistened roller thing for wetting them before sticking them into the case notes. That was a great advance: Campbell's memories of housemanship were strongly flavoured with the taste of glue. He pointed to it.

'Where did that come from?'

'Dr Creech got them for us. I just mentioned it to him one day and they arrived the next.'

Campbell was impressed. He would no more have mentioned a thing like that to Creech than he would have asked him for a half day after a hard receiving night. Perhaps he had underestimated the senior consultant, somehow imagining that had he, as a houseman, made such a suggestion it would have been met with blank disbelief and a lecture about how when Creech had been doing the job forty years ago housemen were expected to boil up their own glue.

Dr Moray, or Jean, as Campbell had immediately begun to think of her, was leaning back in her chair, with her hands behind her head, more in the manner of someone making the most of their bust. She looked Campbell over for a moment then said, 'What's it like to be back?'

'Funny. Distant. The same but different. Sister hasn't changed a bit. Even one or two of Creech's old patients are still there. But it feels different.'

'When were you last here?'

'November.'

'First house job?'

'Yes.'

'Where did you go after that?'

'Ravelston Orr's.'

She did not react to that: most people said either something like 'You poor bugger' or 'They say he's mellowed a lot'.

'Then you were ill or something, weren't you?'

'Yes. For a while. I had to do some surgical locum work to get enough time in to register. That's why I'm starting at a funny time. Sort of out of step.'

'What was wrong with you?'

'The yellow peril.'

'Hepatitis?'

'Yes.'

'All right now?'

'Drinking normally.'

Her face clouded slightly at that. It crossed Campbell's mind that she might be a Wee Free teetotaller. In every year in the medical school there were a few such girls. They sat in the front row, took copious notes, dressed badly and didn't shave their legs. She was not dressed badly. Not well, but not badly either. A pinkish light tweedy skirt and a red and white flowery silk or silkish blouse. And her legs did not have the hairy Christian look which in Campbell's experience betokened piety, smelly armpits and worse. Such girls, moreover, were not often to be found sitting leaning back with their hands behind their heads.

'I don't remember you around the unit as a student,' said Campbell steering things away from an inessential and possibly problematical zone.

'I didn't train here.'

'Where did you train?'

'Aberdeen.'

'Oh.' There were standard things to say about all known medical schools other than God's own. Campbell resisted them. 'How's it working out?'

She smiled as though sensing some incipient, predictable badinage. 'Not too bad. They taught us some medicine. And the language barriers aren't insurmountable.'

'You don't speak Aberdeenish.'

'No . . . I'm from Edinburgh.' She said it with a self-parodying Edinburgh girls' school accent which caused Campbell to break up inside. She was laughing too: there was something innocently irresistible about nice people who laughed at their own jokes. There was a relaxed, enjoyable silence after which she sat forward and looked suddenly thoughtful. 'It must be nearly time for lunch. Do you eat in the general mess?

'I suppose so, now I'm not a resident. Do you? I mean don't you eat in the residency mess?'

'Very rarely. The food's worse, if anything, and usually cold. . . . And it's maybe something to do with not having trained here. . . .' She lowered her voice a little. 'It's boring.'

'What?'

'The residency mess. A lot of men I don't know bitching about consultants I don't know. That is when they're not talking about nurses and how much they drank last night.'

'Oh.' It had not seemed so at the time.

She took off her white coat and turned away to hang it up. As she did so he noticed that the zip at the back of her red and white possibly silk blouse was half an inch down at the top. She turned round again. He opened the door for her and they walked off towards the general mess. Campbell had forgotten he was hungry.

'What else do you do?'

'What do you mean?'

'When you're not looking after Rosamund's female beds. Have you got the men as well?'

'No . . . I'm in research.' Campbell was conscious of using the phrase for the very first time, feeling like someone asking for the station in a brand new language learned from gramophone records.

'What are you doing?'

'Looking for something in gut mucosa. To do with the faecal vitamin pilot study. I think I'm phase two.' He was not sure that he wasn't being quietly mocked. These new languages weren't easy to pick up.

'How's it going?'

'Okay so far. Early days. I just started this morning.'

They queued at the food counter in the general mess. She was in front and Campbell watched her in profile as she chose soup and salad and yoghurt. She was lithe and long-legged and looked as though she was slim because it came naturally and not as a result of stepping nervously on bathroom scales and worrying and eating nasty little meals she didn't enjoy. He chose a more traditional lunch with institutional stodge. Without discussing where to sit they went over and sat at one of the quiet tables by the farthest windows.

Prior to his promotion Campbell had eaten only rarely in the general mess, but by the nature of the Institute and its workings it was full of people he knew. There were doctors from his own year, last year's residents, now in senior house officer posts or research attachments like his own. Registrars and other junior staff tended to eat together by units, and both in the queue and at the tables their little groups of three or four or five could be identified. Some of the younger consultants ate with these groups; the older ones, resisting the enforced democracy of this new dining room (until recently they had had a separate, somewhat lordly establishment with table service and a modest wine cellar), sat gravely in little groups of their own, like great beasts at a waterhole ignoring parrots, monkeys and small game. In the corner farthest from Campbell and the house physician there were tables, distinguished by the suggestion rather than the actual presence of broomsticks and cauldrons, where the senior nursing staff ate and gossiped in hissing covens.

Though the place lacked the now questionable camaraderie of the residency mess, there were certain points in its favour, principally the presence of large numbers of attractive young women : physiotherapists, sleek, alert and fit like sporting dogs or police horses, and tables and tables of nurses, some of whom Campbell knew quite well and quite a few of whom he had known very well indeed, if briefly.

'You're leering,' said Jean. 'Your soup's getting cold.'

Now she really was laughing at him. Campbell managed an embarrassed grin over the first spoonful of brown windsor, and turned his attention once more to the resident. He decided she really was attractive, as attractive as any other girl in the room at the time, not with the kind of loveliness that men fell about over in pubs, just pleasant regular features and a sensible, unemphatic, visibly intelligent niceness that Campbell had hoped for more often than he had found in the girls of his acquaintance. The word 'wholesome', but for its cold-shower and health-food associations, would have done admirably for her.

All the rest of her was nice at least, Campbell concluded halfway through the soup, but her eyes really were beautiful: flecky grey-blue with thick dark lashes and white white whites. (How did she manage that as a houseman?) He wondered momentarily if he had begun to leer at her too and was about to be rebuked once more.

The tables had begun to fill up and there was now a distant risk of additional company. Campbell imagined with dread the arrival of a couple of his own more crass contemporaries, full of tales of nurses and how much they had had to drink last night, and felt helplessly possessive about their quiet table in its pleasant daylit corner. They finished their soup. Campbell started on his stodge, she on her salad. She even ate cheerfully.

'That looks frightfully healthy.'

'I don't usually eat very much at lunchtime. We eat more in the evening.'

The plural pronoun erupted and seemed to treble the width of the wedding ring on the hand holding the fork.

'What does your husband do?'

'He's in research.'

'Medical?'

'Yes. But he's not in human just now.'

'What's he doing?'

'Seasonal behaviour in amphibians.'

'What?'

'What makes frogs have sex.'

'Oh. Really.'

'You don't sound very impressed.'

'I don't know anything about the field. Tell me.'

'It doesn't sound very good. And sometimes people laugh. But it's good basic stuff with a new technique.'

'And what does?'

'What does what?'

'Make frogs have sex.'

'Nobody knows. But my husband will probably find out.'

Campbell ruminated on the wisdom or otherwise of remarking what a privilege it was to be having lunch with the wife of the man who was about to find out what makes frogs have sex. He did not. Wives were funny about their husbands.

'Is he a medical graduate?'

'Aberdeen. Both of us.'

'Is he going back to proper medicine eventually?'

'Yes.'

'What sort of thing?'

'Human reproductive physiology, probably.'

'Is that what he's really interested in?' To his surprise Campbell managed to say that without sounding either arch or salacious.

'That's his real field.' She smiled in a thought provoking way. 'What are you going to do?'

'Membership, I suppose, then be some sort of physician. Probably guts. It's quite an interesting area. All human life is there.'

'Is yours a study job?'

'Didn't sound like one when Rosamund told me about it this morning. But I suppose I'll have time to open the odd book between the clinics and the chronic diarrhoea out-patients and pushing back the frontiers of knowledge.'

'When are you sitting it?'

'I haven't made up my mind yet.'

They finished lunch. As they walked out of the mess a nurse with whom Campbell had once absentmindedly slept gave him a big smile.

'Friend of yours?'

'Used to work with her.'

'Coffee?'

They poured themselves coffee in the lounge then went out, as was the custom on fine days, on to the Institute's only lawn. It was busy. All the deck chairs had been taken and there were groups standing in the sun and others lying out on the grass in rows as though the lawn were a popular beach. The grass was parched and trodden and generously sprinkled with cigarette ends and other litter. Once more they found a quiet, sunny corner. Campbell took off his jacket and spread himself on the grass. The resident stooped to put down her coffee and lay down beside him.

It was warm and curiously holidaylike. The chatter of voices and the sun, bright even through closed eyelids, obliterated the images of hospital. The wail of an ectopic seagull conspired to complete the escape. August for the people. Campbell lay half-pretending he had got away from it all and half-thinking about the house physician who lay beside him. On the grounds that looking at her would be at least as pleasant as thinking about her, he rolled over and began to drink his cup of coffee, which was on the grass between them. She lay supine, with her eyes closed against the sun. Her mouth was a little open and he could see some of her teeth, white and shapely. In front of her ear there was a little patch of short, fine, almost colourless hair. A wisp of dry grass wafted on to her cheek. Without opening her eyes she moved her mouth and chin until the piece of grass fell off again. Campbell felt that quite soon he was going to have to lie face down.

Still without opening her eyes, she said softly, 'And I thought being a houseman was going to be hell.'

'It has its moments.'

'And its other moments.'

She too opened her eyes and blinked a bit then lay half over and started to drink her coffee. Campbell turned to lie on his face, with lust incarnate uncomfortably disposed. There was dry grass in the remains of his coffee. He fished it out and looked at the resident.

If, at that moment, the Institute's clock tower, fifty yards behind them, had collapsed to rubble with a cataclysmic roar, Campbell would not have looked round. The girl lying beside him, of whom he had known nothing at all one hour before, commanded his entire attention as nothing or no one had ever done in the past. Propped up on one elbow, she sipped her coffee in the sun.

'How did you get on with Bill Dempster?' he heard himself

ask in a faint and hoarse voice, to stop himself saying something that might screw things up with her instantly and forever.

She looked at him as though he had asked a very serious question. 'Nice chap. Good doctor. When he's there.'

'Oh?'

'Well, he's got so many irons in the fire. You know, here and at the Southern. And even when he's around the Institute he dots about between Medical Physics and Haematology and Pathology and Rosamund's unit and the University Library.'

As a houseman Campbell had had unconfirmed suspicions about Bill Dempster's use of time. 'What's he going to do now he's shed his clinical responsibilities?'

'Come on. Looking after three patients doesn't take all day. He said Creech had spoken to him about taking some more of the teaching and Rosamund wanted him to get some stuff ready for publication. He seems to be quite busy. And he's presenting something at the joint clinical meeting today.'

'What sort of thing?'

'One of his interesting cases.'

'You going?'

'I thought I might if it's quiet on the ward.'

'I suppose I ought to. Being a big deal Rosamund meeting. How's time?'

'We've got ages,' she said, lying down prone, as he was lying, and facing him. She snuggled her face into her arms and they looked at each other at a remarkably short range across the burnt grass between the coffee cups. She was faintly tanned and there were half a dozen freckles across the bridge of her nose. Campbell was aware of a profound, almost visceral sensation, a wave of anguished ecstasy, a kind of psychological orgasm that left him faint and floating. He swallowed heavily and took a deep breath. She closed her eyes and muttered, 'Wake me if I fall asleep.'

She did not fall asleep. They lay talking sleepily, almost whispering, mainly about the unit and the patients, until it was time to go to the meeting.

At about ten to two they left the lawn and went back into the hospital building. For the first time between them there was a moment of awkwardness, which she resolved by saying,

'Hang about. I'm off to the loo.'

Campbell hung about feeling he would happily wait for days or weeks. As he did so a man who had been a couple of years above him in medical school appeared from nowhere.

'Campbell! How are you? Where have you been? You back in the old pest house permanently? Who are you working for?'

'Sort of permanently. A year in the first instance. For Rosamund.'

'Oh. Clever stuff?'

'Not very.'

'Doing membership?'

'Thinking about it.'

'Getting enough experience?'

'I hope so. By the time I sit it anyway.'

'What about acute experience?'

'Oh, I think I'll be on the receiving registrar rota eventually.'

'What about a bit of intensive care?'

'What?'

'I'm running the rota for the intensive care unit's night cover.'

'Oh.'

'How d'you feel about joining it?'

'Hadn't thought about it.'

'You should. Good experience. You see a useful range of acute stuff. Good to mention when you go for other jobs.'

'I'll think about it.'

'It's more or less expected of all the post-registration people on the medical units.'

'Oh.'

'And my consultant's got agreement in principle from all the senior consultants on the medical corridor.'

'Oh.'

'Including Creech. Shall we say Friday night?'

'Friday?'

'Well, you're fairly junior on the rota, and you'll have to do your share of the bad nights. At least to begin with.'

'Oh all right.'

'Thanks very much. One more on the rota really will help.

You'll be on for Friday then. And about every three weeks after that.'

'Always Fridays?'

The intensive care unit night cover duty rota organiser laughed. 'Of course not. Some Saturdays too, of course. To begin with. Then mainly Monday to Thursday like everybody else.'

'Thanks.'

'Don't mention it. Great to see you back again.' He scribbled something on the back of an X-ray request card and trotted off. Campbell wondered who was next for his effusive greeting.

Jean rejoined him. She had combed her hair too, and seemed to Campbell lovelier than ever. They walked together down to the Old Lecture Theatre and sat at the back. It was as antiquated as the name could suggest, a tiered amphitheatre of dark-stained pine worn smooth by the boredom of generations. The audience that was gathering was a medium-sized half-interested one of the sort that would unthinkingly put itself together for anything labelled 'clinical meeting' in a teaching hospital where it was quite possible to fill up a perfectly respectable thirty-hour week doing nothing else. Campbell had been attending such meetings, man and boy, for about four years. Like his childhood churchgoing, it was an unexamined ritual, with an aura of self-improvement, in which form was more important than content and detailed recollection remained only of the bizarre, as when a visiting lecturer's slides were dropped and hopelessly mixed up, or the minister's top teeth had fallen out in the last line of 'All People That on Earth do Dwell'.

A little troop of Indian post-graduates in thick pullovers and tweedy jackets filed in and occupied the row in front. They took out notebooks and fountain pens and muttered among themselves. A small fat man at the end of the row turned round and looked up towards Campbell.

'Excuse me please, doctor. Can you tell me which please is Sir Rabelton Orr?' he asked, with curried breath.

'Not here yet. And he's not a sir.'

'And which please is the famous Dr Creech?'

'On the left in the front row. White hair.' Campbell forbore to add, 'And he's not famous.' Perhaps he was famous in India.

Jean sat on Campbell's right, closer than was strictly necessary, with her elbows on the ledge in front, looking round at the audience. Half of the front row remained empty, reserved, not by a notice but by a tacit and inalienable tradition, for Rosamund and those who were to present cases at her meeting. Usually she led her party in at three minutes past the hour. Campbell glanced at the clock (the size of a cart wheel, with yellowing face and huge gilt roman numerals) above the blackboard and decided he would spend the remaining two minutes looking at Jean's left forearm if this could be achieved with discretion.

He had just begun to do so when the forearm moved and she nudged him in the ribs then pointed to something scribbled in the pine surface in front of her. Campbell leant across to read it, a manoeuvre that involved putting his head over her shoulder, scenting a couple of intoxicating lungfuls of her and sustaining a near-fatal blow on the side of his face from a wisp of her hair.

The legend she indicated, when Campbell had focused to read it, said :

> O Henry Creech
> We thee beseech
> To cease to preach
> And learn to teach.

Beneath that someone else had written 'Creech Rules OK?' and someone else again 'Fuck Off Henry', but Campbell was fairly sure that the house physician had not drawn his attention to either of those. They shared their amusement closely and conspiratorially in a way that made Campbell feel he was about to melt and freeze simultaneously, and looked up together just in time to catch the eye of the subject of the verse, who was scanning round the audience from his place of honour far below. Again the little conspiracy of amusement flared between them.

'. . . In summary then, an interesting and instructive case

which illustrates the problems still to be met in the everyday treatment of high blood pressure. A difficult and fascinating story with its ups and downs, if you'll pardon the pun, not showing anything that hasn't already been reported in the literature but showing perhaps a relatively unique combination of the complications of anti-hypertensive therapy. The diabetes. . . . The polyneuritis. . . . The various blood problems. . . The haemolytic anaemia and the white cell series problems . . . The postural dizziness with the fall and the fractured femur. The gout of course. The episode of hallucinations and delusions of persecution. The depression and the suicide attempt. And of course perhaps the relatively most unique of our problems here: the optic atrophy leading to near-total blindness. Now Mrs Duguid has kindly agreed to come along to illustrate a few of the clinical features.'

Dempster turned round and opened the double doors under the portrait of Dr Argyll Robertson to admit the patient. A stooped and tremulous porter who had been shuffling round the Institute with undiagnosed Parkinson's disease for as long as Campbell could remember brought Mrs Duguid in. She sat in a wheelchair, cocooned to her neck in a pink blanket. She wore dark glasses.

'Hello, Mrs Duguid,' said Dempster in a loud cheerful voice. The patient turned her face uncertainly towards him and smiled. 'How are you today, Mrs Duguid? It's very good of you to come along to meet these doctors who've all been most interested in your illness. Now if we could just have a look at your hands. . . .'

He unwrapped her. 'Stretch your hands out. That's it. Turn them over. Palms upward. That's it. Thank you, Mrs Duguid. You'll observe the marked wasting of the interosseous muscles and the almost complete absence of the thenar eminence. Thank you, Mrs Duguid. Now if you'll just take off your glasses. . . .' The patient did so, shakily. Dempster stuck a hand about a yard in front of her face, with all the fingers spread out. 'How many fingers am I holding up?'

'Three,' said the patient.

'Well, that seems to be an improvement on last month,' said Dempster loudly to the patient, following it with 'Near total blindness. Static since April' less loudly, over his shoulder to the audience. The patient groped in her lap for her dark glasses.

The Indians scribbled in unison.

'Just one more thing please, Mrs Duguid. Your patellar reflexes.' Dempster ripped the pink blanket from her knees, walked over to the trolley of clinical instruments the pride of which was an old brass cartridge case holding half a dozen tendon hammers. He chose one thoughtfully, like a golfer selecting an iron for a difficult lie, and walked back to the patient flexing its cane shaft.

The patient's legs were thin and yellowish and already fairly well exposed by the brevity of her nightdress. Dempster knelt beside her and put a forearm under one of her knees, lifting her thigh in such a way as to offer the elders on the front bench an inadvertent but generous view of the patient's underwear, if any.

'Just relax, Mrs Duguid.' He tapped her rigid and trembling leg just below the kneecap. Nothing happened. 'Just relax and try to go all floppy. Let me have the weight of your leg.'

The patient did not relax. Dempster tapped away for a few moments like an enthusiastic amateur geologist then abandoned his attempt, standing up and explaining to his audience that when tested on the ward that morning the knee jerks had been present and symmetrical, but diminished.

'Thank you very much for coming along, Mrs Duguid.' He nodded to the porter, who parcelled her up again and whisked her out with a promptitude that was all the more commendable in view of his own major neurological problems. Dempster stood facing his audience with satisfaction if not with pride.

'Any questions?'

'What's her blood pressure?'

'Normal.'

One of the Indians began to clap and was rapidly suppressed by his neighbours. There were no other questions. Dempster returned to the front bench and Rosamund got up to introduce the next speaker. He was a consultant surgeon she had dug out of a country hospital to talk about his vast and obsessionally documented series of surgically treated ulcer patients. His reputation, such as it was, depended on producing overwhelming numerical evidence for things that everyone knew already. He hacked away from year to year among his tolerant and respectful rural clientèle, watching his series grow from three to four figures and turning up from time to time at meetings such as this, and occasionally even at international surgical gatherings, with longer and longer follow-ups and increasingly complicated slides showing ever more massive cohorts of dots, each one of which represented a stomachless citizen.

One of Rosamund's minor technical acolytes took up a position by the slide projector and the lights were dimmed. The speaker stood at a large almost ecclesiastical lectern with a yellowish light illuminating his notes. He spoke softly with a highland accent and used words in a way that suggested he had originally been a Gaelic speaker and had learned English late in life by reading the medical journals.

The dimmed lights and the whirr of the projector, the soft, droning voice and the reassuring familiarity of what, however obscurely, was being said, all combined most soporifically. After one especially soothing phrase about the establishment of statistically significant negative correlations, Campbell's already intermittent concentration lapsed completely, and his attention wandered first round the audience, half-lit though still in the main familiar and recognisable, then to the girl at his side, who was sitting with her long and lovely legs tucked back under the bench, and her arms folded. She had scarcely moved since the beginning of the meeting, which seemed to Campbell a considerable feat of stoicism, given the hard and narrow bench with its calculatedly inadequate Spanish-inquisition legroom. The voice droned on and on. The noise of Jean's breathing, close, soft and regular, was far more interesting and, as he listened to it and glimpsed from the corner of his eye the small recurrent movements of her chest and her breasts and her arm right next to his own, it came to dominate his sensory input, as though they were lying together in a dark and silent bedroom, with him awake and her asleep at his side. He listened, sitting still for as long as he could on the buttock-torturing pine, then moved a little and stretched his legs obliquely. Almost at the same time, Jean did exactly the same thing, then they settled again, like lovers half asleep, breathing in time.

Campbell was desolated: to the near-telepathic rapport of the last couple of hours it seemed there was to be added a physical intuition, an unconsidered, almost symbiotic mutual awareness that Campbell had experienced all too rarely and briefly. Sleepy, infatuated, loving lust enveloped him. The slides came and went. The speaker crooned long quantitative sentences below.

When the lights came up he looked round to find her looking at him. Campbell, who knew all too well what he was thinking himself, wondered what she was thinking, and could not or dared not guess from her face. They looked blankly and helplessly at each other for a few moments, then down towards the front where Rosamund was standing foursquare in the centre of the little semicircular stage, winding up the meeting.

The wooden stairs between the tiers of benches were steep and narrow and as the crowd cleared across the stage and trickled out through the doors behind it Campbell went down a few steps and looked back up towards Jean. As he did so she stumbled forward and he put out a hand which she caught, steadying herself immediately.

'Thanks. Pins and needles. My leg's all numb and wobbly.'
'Careful then.'
'I will.'

They walked slowly back to the wards behind the crowd dispersing along the corridor, very much together but not talking. They were in the duty room again before Campbell realised that he had no particular reason for going there at the time. She reached into the corner where her white coat hung. Once more Campbell noticed her zip, now open a little further.

'You're a bit undone at the back.'
'Do me up then,' she said without turning round, still reaching for her coat.

As Campbell did so, chastely and reverently, Sister walked into the dusty room with a smile indicating immediate assimilation, previous suspicion, qualified tolerance, a strong hint that such indiscretion should preferably occur off the premises, and a guarantee of confidentiality provided it didn't happen again.

'I thought you'd taken the afternoon off, Dr Moray.'

'No.' She looked suddenly aghast and put her hand up to her mouth in schoolgirl remorse. 'Gosh, my bleep.'

'I wondered about that,' said Sister, 'and took the liberty of looking in the pocket of your white coat.'

'Gosh I'm sorry. Has anything happened?'

'Not a lot. I had to get Dr Hamilton up to see to a few things. Nothing important. Was it a good meeting?'

'Quite interesting.'

Sister went back into the ward. Campbell and Jean parted at the door.

'See you tomorrow.'

'See you tomorrow.'

Campbell returned to the research fellows' room. No one else was there. On his desk there was the morning's *Guardian*, with 'Thanks a lot. R.A.' scrawled across the corner, together with the *Financial Times* and the *Scotsman*, which was still folded open at the financial pages, with a lot of stars and underlinings and incomprehensible squiggles annotating the dense columns of share prices. Campbell had a panicky moment, looking round for his notes from the morning session with Rosamund, before finding them under the heap of newspapers.

The secretary was doing her fingernails when he went along again for some paper. She seemed quite pleased to be distracted from the task and they chatted for a little while about the unit in general. She was known to have a monopoly of the more interesting items of gossip – things about jobs, promotion, marriage problems and intra- and inter-unit politics, and time spent in her company was seldom wasted. She dispensed information slowly and with great discrimination, and Campbell felt that even if he did not learn very much from this initial encounter he might at least re-establish the tentative diplomatic accord they had reached before his departure to Ravelston Orr's unit the previous year. He complimented her on her pot plants, and they talked about nothing in particular.

She was not giving much away. Campbell remembered what he had come for and she surprised him by not only providing him with two packets of foolscap but throwing in some felt-tipped pens as well.

'Have you taken over Dr Fyvie's female beds from Dr Dempster?'

'Yes.'

'I hope you'll be a bit quicker than he was about dictating your letters.'

'Why? Wasn't Bill?'

'Look at that. Discharge summaries awaiting dictation. Dr Fyvie's female patients.' It was an impressive heap considering there were only three or four beds.

'Apparently he's been very busy.'

'Maybe busy. Or distracted.'

'Research?'

She snorted.

'Teaching?'

She snorted again.

'His kids?'

She did not snort. Campbell felt he was getting warm.

'Family problems?'

'Call it family.' She picked up her nail file and returned to her manicure.

'Thanks for the paper. And the pens.'

'Any time. Just drop in.'

Campbell went back to his desk. There was another item on it: a typed list with one of Rosamund's 'With Compliments' slips initialled by her secretary and stapled to the top corner. It listed references relevant to his field of research, culled from journals he knew about, like the *Lancet*, journals he had heard of, like the *Journal of the American Medical Association*, and some totally obscure middle European publications from which, it was devoutly to be hoped, translations would be available. There were about fifty items and a quick scan through the titles did little to fire Campbell's enthusiasm for his proposed year's work.

'Phytamenadione-induced mutagenesis in foetal rat colonic fibroblasts: a preliminary report of *in vitro* studies.' 'Aberrant karyotypes in vitamin depleted mammalian colon: a new hypothesis for colonic carcinogenesis.' 'Vitamin degradation products and antibiotic-induced colonic recolonisation.' 'Faecal vitamins: another clue in the cancer complex?' The question mark suggested to Campbell that that particular author suspected they weren't.

The list brought home a realisation of his broad ignorance of the field and he asterisked a few of the more accessible-looking general articles with a view to spending the rest of the afternoon in the university medical library acquiring a preliminary overview. There would be time enough to get into the Hungarian literature later. He ripped the blue paper from his first packet of foolscap.

'Hello, David.'

Campbell turned round. A fair-haired man a few years older than himself was hanging up a neatly pressed linen jacket and putting on a lab coat.

'You settling in then?'

'Yes.'

'I suppose you really know enough about how the unit works to feel at home right away.'

'Yes.' Campbell decided his assailant was a Fraser somebody who had been a shadowy figure on the research periphery of the unit when he had been toiling at the coalface of house-manship a year before.

'Awfully nice you're back. I must say I was pleased when I heard you'd got the job. Lots of competition I expect?'

'Some.' One other candidate had been offered the job. Then he had died.

'How's it coming along then? I expect you're brimming with ideas. All ready to get down to some really solid experimental work.'

'I've only just begun.'

'That's always the hardest bit.'

'Yes.' A few more details about the man surfaced: Fraser Ratho, whose father and grandfather and uncles and cousins seemed to have had success in medicine as a hereditary trait; one of the great dynasties. Campbell had wondered once how the shades of previous Rathos – clinicians, heavy-weight medical politicians, academics famed and feared as external examiners from Cape Town to Hong Kong – looked down on this genteel contemporary disappointment.

'Have you been for tea?'

Campbell noticed that Ratho had white paint under his fingernails and on his hands. There was a little on his insufferably buoyant blond hair too.

'Not yet.'

'We usually go to the sister's room in the male ward.'

Campbell remembered all too well the ravages regularly committed on the male ward's teatime sandwiches by underemployed research staff. He felt hungry again.

'By the way,' said Ratho as they walked along the corridor, 'I wonder how you'd feel about seeing a few patients for me tomorrow afternoon. You'll probably remember some of them from the ward when you were there. It's Dr Creech's Thursday colitis clinic actually. I greatly look forward to it but unfortunately can't manage tomorrow's. There aren't many patients booked but it might be useful experience.'

'How many?'

'Three.'

'I've never had anything to do with that clinic.'

'It's quite straightforward. If they've been having diarrhoea, you double the dose of salazopyrine. If they're constipated, you just give them a wee holiday from the tablets.'

'And if they're all right?' enquired Campbell, just to see what he would say.

'Oh, I should just keep them on the same dose if I were you. Provided there aren't any contra-indications.'

'Okay.'

'Thanks ever so. . . . You won't have met the new house physician down here. Dr Hamilton. She's awfully good.'

'Two female residents?'

'Yes.' He giggled. 'Dr Creech was feeling a little adventurous.'

Dr Hamilton turned out to be one of the cleverest, largest and ugliest female medical graduates Edinburgh had produced for some time. And there were no sandwiches left. Old Creech himself and Bertram, one of his registrars, appeared, followed shortly afterwards by fresh tea and another plate of sandwiches. Creech was in benign form, and positively beaming towards his former resident. 'You'll know everybody. Just make yourself at home. If you want paper or anything like that go along to the unit secretary. Come and see me if there's anything you think I could help you with. Books. . . . References. . . . That sort of thing. Take your time and settle in. Don't go rushing at things you haven't read up on and thought about. Take it easy for a wee while at least.'

'Yessir.'

'How are you feeling now anyway?'

'Fine, sir.'

'I've had it too you know. . . . In Burma. . . .' They went through all that, not for the first time and he eventually got round to a story Campbell hadn't heard before about a chindit who swallowed the top of his water-bottle. It passed the time quite pleasantly. The houseman waddled out halfway through the tale, making it clear to Campbell at least that however bright she was she would not survive long in the highly competitive world of teaching hospital medicine. Campbell, Ratho and Bertram listened politely.

'. . . So when it turned up eventually, so to speak . . . proving his point, they dropped the charge of losing it and changed it to one of rendering it unfit for use instead. The man . . . I remember his name now, it was McCormack . . . a nasty wee man . . . wanted to argue that one too, but as the unit's medical officer I really had to put my foot down.'

Bertram smiled diplomatically. Campbell waited for Ratho to say something like 'Ho ho, sir. Ho ho ho,' but was disappointed.

Creech got up to go and Bertram went with him, which was a pity because he was one of the few people around the place that Campbell had been looking forward to seeing again. He was an enlightened cynic who practised medicine well because he liked it, and did his various bits of research passably because the constraints of the system compelled it. He had a sense of the absurdity of it all and his own absurdity within it, which made him good company in a unit where insight was at a premium.

When they had gone, Ratho said, 'Thank you very much for taking on that clinic tomorrow. . . . It might be better not to mention it to Rosamund or Dr Creech or even Dr Bertram for that matter. After all, your primary commitment is to research.'

Back in the research fellows' room once more, Ratho took off his lab coat, put on his linen jacket and left. Campbell sat alone in the room, looking out of the window. The view was not unpleasant, and included some trees, green and heavy with late-summer leaves, a broad walk leading to the park, and the back of a Georgian terrace which formed one side of a square. There were more trees in the square, so that the view was mostly green. In the shaded avenue of the walk, pedestrians came and went in summer ease: schoolboys with their jackets off, swinging satchels at each other; young mothers with prams; an old lady with a fat dog, both looking a bit too warm. After a few minutes Ratho, cutting a slightly passé figure with his light old-fashioned jacket and his Rupert Brooke hairstyle, strolled past whistling. He looked up at the window. Campbell waved, but Ratho looked quickly away and did not acknowledge him.

The *Financial Times* proved to cover many things other than finance. Its review section was positively catholic and its general news, lucid and quite free from shocks, probes and vicars, offered a useful and orthographic complement to his morning's reading of the *Guardian*. Campbell pondered for some time the problem of why it was pink, a distinction it shared, to the best of his knowledge, only with the sporting editions of an obscure evening newspaper he never read.

By half past four it was too late to go over to the university medical library to commence his reading programme. Instead he finished opening his packets of foolscap and stowed it neatly in the top left-hand drawer, took a stroll round the other desks and borrowed a paper clip to attach two blank sheets to his notes from the meeting with Rosamund, so as to be ready to expand on them in the morning, and on another sheet made a short list of the various things he had meant to do that day, beginning with his proposed self-teaching programme on problems in diagnosis and management of primary biliary cirrhosis and ending with a memo to himself about the review articles in Rosamund's list of references. Creech's remark about not rushing into things seemed, on further consideration, sound advice.

Between half past four and quarter to five, one or two more of Campbell's fellow tenants of the desks in the room

drifted in and out. A girl, the one from whom in her absence
Roddy Abavana had suggested he borrow some paper, came
in with a full shopping bag and a carrier bag from a department store. A fresh-looking, red-faced man burst in and
grabbed a cricket bag from behind the coat stand and rushed
out again. Bill Dempster, who turned out to be a near neigh-
bour in the room, came in and sat on Campbell's desk for a
while and talked about his commitments. Campbell realised
that in a perfectly ordered world he would have gone round
the ward with his predecessor on taking over the beds. He
said something to that effect.

'Sorry, David. Helluva busy. Had to prepare that case for
Rosie's big meeting. Otherwise I would have done. I thought
about it. Could do it tomorrow sometime.'

'Not much point. I've been round. It seems okay. Mrs
Herron, maybe.'

'Booked.'

'Really?'

'Almost certainly. Nothing else it could be. Nothing that I
can think of anyway. Feel free to prove me wrong though.'

Campbell was aware of an almost overwhelming temptation
to turn the conversation to the subject of the more junior
medical staff on the ward, so that he could think aloud about
her and hear someone else talking about her and saying her
name. Instead he said, 'I thought your case went very well.'

'Thanks. It was hard luck about her knee jerks. They were
lovely this morning.'

'Tough.'

'Sometimes they get stage fright. Particularly with tendon
reflexes. There's not a damned thing you can do. Nice muscle
wasting in her hands though.'

'Yes.'

There was a pause then Dempster said, 'You've got a good
resident up there.'

'The girl? Dr . . .'

'Jean Moray.'

'She seems okay.'

At half past six that evening, after a fast, risky drive south
from Edinburgh in Hadden's car, Campbell, Hadden and an

anaesthetist whom Campbell had not previously met sat drinking in a Northumberland pub. The anaesthetist, a newcomer to the Institute, was describing a morning in the theatre with Ravelston Orr. Campbell and Hadden, who had worked together under that surgeon and were all too familiar with his little ways, listened to the stranger's views with interest.

'You know the way he trumpets and brays.' The narrator stuck his chin out and grimaced in a fair imitation of his subject. ' "It ill becomes the calling of a surgeon to be found in his operating theatre throwing pieces of his patients around like a keeper feeding sealions at Corstorphine," were his exact words. Then he said, "The cause of patient care can hardly, eh, be said to be advanced by offering half-inch cubes of human flesh for sacrifice on the, eh, altar of science. Get out of my theatre." Then he said "Get out!" a couple of times more, but the fellow kept on and on, saying things like "She'll never miss it," and "Every other surgeon on the corridor takes a more reasonable view," which upset him a bit. He said something about lapses from grace on the part of his colleagues being of no interest to him, whether as argument, persuasion or mere gossip. Then he roared "Get out!" again a couple of times and cut Theatre Sister's finger.'

'I'm afraid that really set him off. He threw his knife at the hatch. It missed and stuck in the surround. The fellow was still there, peering through the hole like a passenger in a stage coach being attacked by redskins and Ravelston Orr was jumping up and down making a terrible noise with his rubber boots and his shouting. Sister got a bit hysterical and one could simply see the staff nurses and student nurses and so on thinking things. Fortunately I was able to keep the patient asleep, so decorum was maintained after a fashion. It did occur to me that he might go away if we gave him a bit of Sister's finger, but no one seemed in the mood for compromise. So one didn't say anything.'

Campbell put down his pint so that he could laugh without spilling it. Hadden was laughing and drinking at the same time. He emptied his glass and said, 'That one hardly touched the sides. Anyone for another.' Neither the anaesthetist nor Campbell said no, and Hadden went over to the bar.

'Was this chap an Australian?'

'Or a Rhodesian. Or possibly a cockney. I can never tell.'

'Sounds like a chap I met in nine and ten theatre this morning. McSomething. McGavigan. Thin chap. On the muscle zinc programme.'

'He mentioned zinc. It didn't seem to mean much to the great surgeon.'

The anaesthetist, whose name Campbell had not caught when Hadden had introduced them an hour before, was a short, neat man with highly polished brogues, cavalry twill trousers, a muted brown check sports jacket and a club tie. He was drinking almost as quickly as Hadden. Campbell hastened to catch up. Hadden returned with three more pints.

'Sorry. The inner man must be attended to. You were saying. . . .'

'Only that Ravelston Orr got more and more worked up about the whole thing, and finally charged over to the hatch. I must admit I worried for a moment about the fellow on the other side. What his blood group was if it came to the bit. That sort of thing. But there was to be no more violence. He fumbled with the hatch and cursed it loose and just before it slammed down there was a pathetic wail from the other side: "But I haven't had a bit for nearly a month." '

They all laughed, for a variety of reasons, and the anaesthetist said, 'I was a bit taken aback. I'd heard of him, of course, but everyone says he's mellowed.'

'Age shall not weary him . . .' Hadden intoned, 'nor custom stale his infantile barbarity.'

Then he called his secretary to the hatch and dictated a letter to the board of management. Peppery stuff about nebulously attached research personnel, presumably belonging to the medical profession, comporting themselves around his operating theatre like mongrels outside a butcher's.'

'Thanks for the warning,' said Campbell, who had no notion for such an encounter with his old surgical chief.

'Are you in the hunt too, David?' the anaesthetist enquired, making Campbell feel more guilty about forgetting his name.

'In a small way.'

'Muscle?'

'No, gut. Large gut.'

'Which particular frontier of science are you pushing forward?'

'Something on vitamins.'

'Yes, young Campbell, explain yourself,' Hadden commanded. 'What was a sensible chap like you doing in that row of idiots up there this morning? A crossword puzzle?'

'No. I told you. Looking for a bit of large gut. I thought there was a case. It died, you said.'

'Tut, tut. Perhaps he didn't know you cared. Did you manage to locate a substitute contributor?'

'No. It was a quiet morning on the research front.'

'I'm glad to hear it. Who's paying you anyway?'

'Rosamund has some spare money floating around. From a drug company, actually.'

'So? A hireling of the bloated capitalists battening on the sufferings and credulity of the masses?'

'That sort of thing.'

'How much?'

'About the same as I got last year.'

'What's in the job?'

'Well, I'll be doing some of this research thing, a bit of clinical work, some teaching . . . and I hope to get some reading done for membership.'

'That sounds like the brochure. Where does it get you?'

'I don't know.'

'Come on. Where d'you think it's getting you?'

'A few publications maybe. And it'll keep me in play . . . in case anything more interesting turns up.'

'Such as?'

'I don't know. But membership might not be a bad thing.'

'What for?'

To show that nihilism was not the sole prerogative of surgical registrars Campbell replied, 'So the world will know I've read a book or two since leaving medical school. Unlike eighty per cent of the brethren. How's surgery?'

'Okay. A bit dull after Ravelston Orr. Inevitably. But okay.'

'Who are you with?'

'That bunch in nine and ten. McElwee, Fordyce and Blair. Piles, hernias and veins. With bellies and breasts as a treat.

Classic general drudgery.'

'What are they like? McElwee always struck me as a bit of a cretin.'

'Bertie? A sort of bald, bad-tempered, bow-tied baby of fifty-four. Halfway through a long case he'll stamp his feet — and say "Bertie-wertie wants a drinkie-winkie," and he won't be happy until he gets it. Only orange juice, mind. It's a little wearing and you can't do anything but put up with it, but it's better than the sturm and drang of yesteryear at the court of the Mad Mullah of Morningside. Bertie's not that bad. You should go and ask him nicely about giving you your little pieces of people. He'd like that. Having someone else to patronise.'

'Thanks. I will.' Another unmissable thing to do tomorrow.

'Fordyce is your smooth commercial surgeon who thinks the better streets in Edinburgh are paved with gallstones and golden guineas. And little Blairs are seen and not heard. Maybe I mean seen and not listened to. It could all be much, much worse.'

'Much cutting?'

'While Fordyce is carving up the rich man in his castle, I have a nibble at the poor man at his gate. In fact I do most of his NHS lists. And overall it's one of the busier surgical units in the Institute. Bagged a stomach, a thyroid and a breast this morning.'

'There was a girl up there this morning who wanted some of the breast.'

'Yes. La Smith. She's been making a bit of a nuisance of herself. Bertie encourages her. Pats her shoulder and calls her She-who-must-be-obeyed.'

The pub was small and cosy and quite unlike the pubs in Scotland. Hadden sprawled on a worn settee, with the anaesthetist and Campbell in armchairs on each side of him round an empty fireplace with a pale embroidered firescreen standing in front. On the mantelpiece was a radio playing brass band music and a china dog sitting staring soulfully through the radio and along the mantelpiece to the spot at the other end where its lost mate's place had been taken by a 1953 Coronation biscuit tin. An old man with a leathery red-brown neck and a head as bald and white as a baby mushroom sat on a stool at the bar with his back to them.

The anaesthetist got up and walked over towards the back of the pub and a black-painted door with a ceramic figure of a man in evening dress nailed on it.

'Sorry. What's his name again?'

'Baird-Brown,' said Hadden. 'I thought you'd forgotten.'

'Christian name?'

'Anthony.'

'Not Tony?'

'Anthony.'

'Where'd he train?'

'Thomas's.'

'London?'

'As far as I'm aware St Thomas's, Newport Pagnell, hasn't got a medical school.'

'Okay. Is he typical?'

'He may even be what's known as a typical Tommy's type. But I haven't met many.'

'What's he doing here? . . . Not that he's not a decent bloke.'

'Dunno. Ask him.'

When he came back, Campbell did.

'Various reasons,' said Baird-Brown. 'Good idea to get away from the place you started. I'm surprised more of you up here don't. You seem to sort of stay around. The ones who stay around longer get promoted, and the ones who stay around longest of all end up as consultants. . . . But most of us move around a bit.'

'Why the Institute?'

'In case I wanted to go back. It's the only hospital north of the Middlesex anyone's heard of. They all say "Oh, the Institute," and dement a bit about old Sir Wullie McSomething who took them through their first gastrectomy and who'd trained up here when Hippocrates was a houseboy.'

'Are you planning to go back?'

Baird-Brown pursed his lips in a tactful pause. Campbell hoped his question had not sounded inhospitable.

'I expect so. In due course. Eventually. No rush.'

'How d'you find it?'

'The gasman's trade's the same the whole world over. The patients don't have much to say. But the surgery up here's interesting. Relatively speaking, a lot of acute stuff. Old-fashioned too, in some ways. They do piles here with a thing we had in the museum.'

'You from London?' His accent was unplaceably and unashamedly public-school.

'Tommy's.'

'No. I meant do you come from London.'

'No. Up here actually. My father has a practice in one of these awful mining places.'

After three pints Hadden got up and went off to the phone. He came back and said, 'It's all fixed up.'

'What is?'

'Dinner.'

'Where?'

'Back across the border. Only just. Ma Watters'. I've said we'll be there about half past eight. How about a walk?'

That turned out to be another short car journey followed by a bloated breathless stride along a windswept beach under a castle. As they walked across the hard, rippled flats of moist sand Campbell found his mind filling up with Jean again: predictable, rather silly things about her being there, a bit breathless and laughing, with her hair blowing around, instead of the two characters he was actually with, who were pleasant enough in themselves, but not by any means her. He found himself wondering what precisely she was doing at twenty-three minutes past seven on a sunny Wednesday evening, and remembered what she had said about eating a bigger meal in the evening; then he went on to imagine a two-way hard-day-at-the-office conversation over the spaghetti bolog. or steak and kidney pudding or whatever, concerning respectively primary biliary cirrhosis and what makes frogs have sex.

Hadden and Baird-Brown were talking about the theory underlying the sacrament of confession, or rather shouting about it over the wind. From what they were saying Campbell confirmed Hadden's black-humoured atheism, and diagnosed in Baird-Brown a form of Catholicism, not orthodox but tending towards Jansenism and almost as depressive in its general import as Hadden's familiar dour philosophy. They walked past the castle and along under a natural barricade of tufted dunes reinforced at intervals by huge concrete cubes, then found their way barred by the broad and slimy estuary of a stream. Hadden looked down at it for a few moments then remarked, 'Even the weariest river winds somewhere safe to sea.'

They did not attempt to cross it but struck inland through the dunes then headed back along the landward ramparts of the castle. There was a little shrine in the wall, a bemused madonna under glass, more appropriate to some continental fortification than to this bleak protestant shore. Again they stopped and Baird-Brown stepped forward and craned to read the inscription.

'If you haven't got a candle I'll lend you a match,' said Hadden.

To Campbell's surprise Baird-Brown produced a rosary and dropped down on to his knees on the grass, looking up to the incarcerated blue and white figure. Campbell wondered if he were doing it from a desire to shock, or from some simple or other piety, and stood sheepishly with Hadden until he had finished.

There was some time in hand before dinner across the border. As they drove back to the pub Campbell thought it would be a good thing to buy the old man there a drink. He had gone. The radio gave forth on greyhound racing. They drank two more pints before heading north.

'You can bring your rosary, Brideshead, but it might be better to leave your Teddy bear in the car.'

Baird-Brown got out of the front seat, looking a little sleepy, and they made their way into Ma Watters' establishment. Her public bar, only a few miles over the border, was intransigently Scottish, a grubby and joyless monument to institutionalised sin, permitted but not rendered enjoyable. There were a few stools and one kitchen table with shaky-looking bentwood chairs. The linoleum was old and worn and the bar top awash with spilt beer. A dartboard in one corner was the only even moderately well-lit object in the room. For the rest, there was gloom modified a little by the light from three small greasy, smoke-darkened windows, which left an almost deliberate obscurity, as though to protect the denizens of the place from too clear a view of each other, lest they should scatter like infernal creatures fleeing from the sight of their own kind. It seemed an unlikely place to have dinner.

'That's Albert,' said Hadden, indicating a stooped barman, who had half-acknowledged their entry. A strong-smelling man with string round the bottoms of his trousers got up and lurched over to the toilet door, casting suspicious eyes around his fellow drinkers and back to a heap of dead rabbits under his chair. Three young men with red faces and high cheekbones, farm workers, to judge from their clothes and the state of their boots, fell silent as Hadden moved past them to the bar.

'Hello, doctor.'

'Hello, Albert. . . . We're a bit early. Can we have a drink in here first?'

'Down the end, doctor.' He nodded to the left, where, in a little alcove receding behind the corner of the bar, was another table, a low, glass-topped affair with an ashtray, and four upholstered chairs.

'This way to the cocktail bar,' said Hadden. They sat down and he ordered three gin and tonic, some peanuts and a jar of pickled onions. The farm workers muttered darkly among themselves and the man who had gone to the toilet came out again, still adjusting his dress, looking round the bar for such signs as suspicious bulges, or little floppy ears or furry paws protruding from pockets. He picked up his rabbits, counting them as he did so, and went out. Campbell wondered what was on the menu.

'D'you come here often?' Baird-Brown enquired airily of Hadden, engendering another round of dark speculation from the rustics.

'Did a GP's locum up the road last year between jobs. Lived in his house and ate down here. I was probably the best fed migrant labour in Europe.'

'Very kind of you to say so, doctor.' Albert put down the drinks and small eats. 'Shall I just add it all in?'

'Yes please.'

'Ma will be along shortly. She has another party, as it happens.'

Albert was stooped and sallow. He spoke with an accent

not dissimilar to Baird-Brown's, and there was much in his manner to suggest that he had not spent all his days serving pints to paranoid poachers. When he had gone Campbell asked Hadden about him.

'Calls himself Major Watters in the phone book. Genuinely I think. But he lays on the Jeeves thing a bit thick when there's company.'

Baird-Brown had some peanuts but no pickled onions. Hadden ate most of them, with Campbell taking a token few.

About halfway through the second round of drinks a very large lady in a sweeping green evening dress approached Hadden from behind, put her hands over his eyes, kissed the top of his head and said, 'Darling! Guess who?'

'Ma!' Hadden leapt to his feet and embraced her. Campbell and Baird-Brown, feeling themselves to be in the presence of no ordinary waitress, stood up too, and were introduced by Hadden as Dr Campbell and Dr Baird-Brown.

'Lovely, lovely to have *all* of you, boys. I was *so* pleased when Graham rang. . . . Graham darling, I haven't seen you for *ages*. How *have* you been?' She pinched Hadden's cheek. 'Have you been working *too* hard? You surgeons! Such marvellous people. But you all work *so* hard.' Her glance embraced Baird-Brown and Campbell. 'Is everyone a surgeon? Do we have a surgical *trio* to dine?'

Campbell explained that Baird-Brown was an anaesthetist and that Campbell was at present engaged in medical research. Anaesthetics had no great impact but she fairly gushed over Campbell's role in life.

'The very *forefront*! All those marvellous breakthroughs. And you're so *young*!' Campbell coughed modestly by way of explaining that he had not personally discovered penicillin or disentangled DNA, but would endeavour to make the most of any such opportunities that came his way. Her smile of studied admiration faded and her attention switched suddenly to a large card she was holding in front of her like an oratorio score. 'I expect you're all starving!'

Hadden smiled. 'What have you got?'

'I've done a trolley of hors d'oeuvres. Mainly sea things, of course, with everything so near and so handy. Then for fish there's lobster or sole. No . . . Sorry. The other lot had all the lobsters. So you'll all be on the meuniere, a wise choice. It's very good this evening. And how about filet de boeuf Wellington?' She made much of pronouncing the general's name in the correct, French way. They all nodded. 'Then another trolley? Things Graham likes. Your favourite mousse?' She arched her eyebrows at Hadden, smiled enormously and swept away.

To Campbell's surprise, her performance appeared to have gone quite unnoticed by the farm workers, who were now playing darts. Baird-Brown sipped his drink and looked to Hadden for some explanation or reaction, but he offered none. Instead he speared the last pickled onion. Campbell got up and slid past Baird-Brown's chair to go to the loo.

When he came back there were three fresh glasses of gin and tonic. A middle-aged woman with fierce gipsy features and greying hair came in, spoke briefly to one of the darts players and led him out by the elbow. He went uncomplainingly and the other two carried on with their game.

Albert reappeared with a wine list, and Hadden ordered one bottle of Chablis and two of a nondescript claret, remarking that pickled onions always made him thirsty. The three sat drinking quietly. Campbell worried about his liver.

Eventually Albert nodded gravely from a door at the other end of the bar, and they moved to the dining-room. It was a big room, almost as big as the bar they had just left, and was decorated in a style of heavy rural elegance, with a maroon carpet, maroon velvet curtains and pink and red flock wallpaper. The three tables, one occupied, one unset and one waiting for their party, were all different, and no more than two of the chairs were alike. Ma Watters' two trolleys stood to one side.

She made another of her entrances and after further exchanges with Hadden the meal began. Ma's role combined those of waitress, hostess, mother, madam and diva: she fluttered and swooped round the tables, alternating between moments of steely efficiency with plates, cutlery, sauceboats and the like, and intervals of urbane expansiveness in which she effortlessly coaxed her guests to eat and drink and talk a little more and a little better, as though the whole thing were an elaboate knife-and-fork exercise at some weird finishing school.

Albert continued with his Jeeves impression, handling the wines with ceremony and aplomb in moments stolen from the service of an increasingly noisy public bar next door. Campbell, Hadden and Baird-Brown ate well and drank very well indeed. The sole was as good as promised and the steak succulent and crisply armoured. Hadden's favourite mousse transpired to be a schoolboy's dream of rich frothed chocolate drowned in cream.

They finished sitting sleepily in a small lounge over coffee and brandy. Baird-Brown, having been silent for some time, became suddenly intense and sat forward in his chair, talking not so much to the others as over and past them.

'If ever good eating were to be proscribed, and its devotees hounded and persecuted, they would gather in rooms like these, small shrines in unexpected places, to keep the old rites alive.'

'What?'

'Chefs would be smuggled in from the continent. The wealthy old families would have secret dining rooms built into their homes. Commissars with buckets of mince and potatoes might rampage through the kingdom but a vast silent network of clandestine cuisine would keep the candle of civilisation alight.' He paused for brandy. 'I envisage Major and Mrs Watters here risking their lives nightly that such as we might eat in the full magnificence of the old way, while peasants roister in their swill next door, unwittingly providing the perfect façade for their sacred mission.' His voice rose and his eyes were staring. He gripped a spoon and gazed at his own small inverted image in it. 'I see a victory over the forces of mediocrity and assimilation. Not a triumph but a quiet stemming of the awful advance of plastic doughnuts and grey faceless tea. . . . For the few and the brave, I see an excellence heightened and enhanced by risk and the fraternity of illicitude. Persecution . . . like the flames of the refiner's fire, will strengthen the strong and winnow the chaff from the seed and the stony ground . . . of a dull, hostile. . . .'

He got up and staggered forward, then dropped on to his knees, much as he had done before the madonna earlier in the evening. Hadden swallowed the last of his brandy and stood up. 'Oh dear. The Blessed Anthony performs again. Find Ma and write her a cheque. You'll get our shares tomorrow. I'll get this pious heap out to the car and we'll start for home.'

Campbell found Ma and wrote a cheque, which extended his powers of concentration and co-ordination more than anticipated. He rounded it up to the nearest five pounds, from gratitude and in the expectation of some carpet cleaning, and as he handed it over mumbled something about the strain of Baird-Brown's work. She said, 'I think he's the first anaesthetist I've met, apart from professionally, of course. Lovely to see you all anyway.'

Baird-Brown was bundled into the back seat, where he curled up clutching his rosary, and Campbell sat in the front seat beside Hadden. Ma Watters and Albert waved them off from the door.

'He'd probably be happier lying straight out on his back with his arms folded across his chest and his feet crossed,' said Hadden. 'I'm sure he sleeps that way, if not in his coffin like those gloomy Cistercian buggers.'

He drove fast and, in the circumstances, reasonably well along a quiet coast road. After a few miles he said, 'It's time we all had some fresh air,' and turned off down a bumpy track towards the sea. The car came to rest in a rough car park overlooking a bay bounded at each end by steep cliffs. Campbell and Hadden got out. The sea was calm and the wind had dropped. A half moon high over the sea lit cliffs, beach, car park, dunes and the track leading down from the main road. Hadden opened a back door and Baird-Brown slumped out half awake and stumbled to his feet. He slammed the door. 'Never mind locking it,' said Hadden. There was no one else around, no other car, only a few darkened chalets behind the car park. The three walked the last few yards down to the beach and set off to the left and out towards the sea.

The tide was far, far out but the sand was still wet. There were shallow pools that they avoided at first, then ignored, splashing through them with a drunken disregard for footwear. If they were walking in any particular direction, it was towards the moon, down a huge, blue-silver rippled flare path above which the half moon hung at top dead centre. It seemed as good a place as any to go. When the puddles became more or less continuous they turned to the left and headed along the beach again.

Baird-Brown was explaining to Hadden the difference between the Virgin Mary and Astarte and Diana and a number of other goddesses whose names Campbell did not recall having heard before, but whose personalities, similarities and differences seemed to mean much to Hadden. Campbell squelched along trying at first to listen then fell back a bit as he thought once more of Jean, remembering how they had lain together on the grass, basking in the sun of early afternoon, with their eyes sometimes open and sometimes closed, talking quietly and unhurriedly as though they had been doing so for years and would continue to do so for the whole of the foreseeable future. He remembered her hands, and her nails, which had been less than entirely clean, but on her, still lovely, and the way she had screwed up her face and moved it around to shake off the bit of grass that had landed on her cheek. Her voice came out of the faint sound of the sea, and over the receding voices of Hadden and Baird-Brown, saying 'I'm from Edinburgh' and 'You're leering, your soup's getting cold'. The way her hair had fallen over her fingers, when she had been sitting at her desk with her hands behind her head, came back to him in vivid detail though he could not remember even noticing it at the time. Her particular laugh, another hallmark of her Edinburgh girls' school conditioning, came suddenly into his mind and made him want to laugh too, alone on the all but deserted beach.

Now far ahead, Hadden and Baird-Brown, the larger figure waving its arms a bit and the smaller shaking its head, walked on in a monochrome long shot of silent film argument. Towards the end of the bay the beach became less flat, with clumps of shaggy boulders surrounded by pools, and larger outcrops spreading from the foot of the cliff. On the seaward side of one of these, two parallel lines of black stumps between three and six feet high rose from the sand like the ribs of a large, mutilated, blackened and half-buried skeleton. Campbell walked between the ribs and stopped. The rows were about eighty feet long and fifteen or twenty feet apart, and not, on closer inspection, parallel, but curving together slightly towards the ends. Somewhat later than he would have cared to admit had he subsequently described the scene to someone else, Campbell realised that he was standing among the last vestiges of a shipwreck, perhaps that of a large fishing boat or a small coaster of wooden construction, whose keel must be buried below his feet, and whose sides and decks and superstructure must have long since been ripped away by storm and tide.

At one end there was a rough pillar, thicker than the ribs and about six feet high, standing right in the centre line. Campbell walked up to it and put a hand on it. It was rough and moist with molluscs and dense fibrous seaweed, and regular in shape: a hollow vertical cylinder with various ports and slots up and down its length, emerging from a larger but shorter horizontal cylinder lying fore and aft and almost completely buried in the sand below. It was the engine, one of the saddest things Campbell had ever seen.

He stood with one hand on it, then leant against it and looked along the beach towards the cliff. Under it the two figures, the Walrus and the Carpenter, turned and started back towards him. It was half past midnight. He thought of Jean, now doubtless asleep against her husband, the man who was probably going to find out what makes frogs have sex, then remembered that his real interest was in human reproductive physiology.

Hadden and Baird-Brown came back along the beach. Hadden was waving and shouting something that Campbell could not make out. They came closer and he shouted it again.

'M'sieur! M'sieur! Défense de pisser sur la machine!'

TWO

'Hello.'

'Hello.'

'Long time no see.'

'Ages.'

'How are you?'

'Okay.'

'No. Really how are you?'

'Fine. Really.'

'I mean after being ill and all that.'

'Okay now. Perhaps a bit frail today. Got smashed last night.'

'Mmm. You don't look too marvellous.'

'You do.'

'I don't. Not straight off a night.'

'Are you? Where?'

'Intensive Care.'

'Really. I'm duty there tomorrow night. You on?'

'No. Nights off.'

'Oh. That would have been nice.'

'What would?'

'To see you again. Will you be going back there after nights off?'

'Yes. For a while.'

'I got grabbed yesterday for that rota. Mostly Fridays and Saturdays for a while, he said.'

'So our Dr Green found you. He said he'd heard you'd turned up again and thought you could be volunteered.'

'It was more like being pressganged. But knowing you're

there makes it all right again.'

She gave him a look familiar from the days when they had been going out together, meaning, I don't believe you but thanks and I know what you're up to. Campbell recognised it with pleasure and they both relaxed a lot.

'Jim said you're working for Rosamund.'

'Yes.'

'What are you doing?'

'I haven't a clue. I spent nearly ten minutes yesterday trying to work it out. I thought I might have another go today.'

'You haven't left yourself much time this morning.'

'I slept in. After last night's full power trial of my liver. Anyway Creech said I should take it easy at first and not rush into things.'

'Mmm. Yes . . . But half past ten. . . .'

'What are you doing still up anyway? I thought little night nurses had to scuttle home before cock-crow or they all turned into parking meters.'

'What? . . . Oh.' She giggled and Campbell remembered why he had begun to go out with her in the first place. 'No. I was shopping.'

'D'you still live over there?'

'Yes. . . . Where are you now you're a retired resident living out?'

'Over there. Marchmont Terrace. I share with Bones.'

'Is he back too?'

'Yes. Thoracic.'

She did not look tired. She just looked normal, in jeans and a sweater, carrying an armful of groceries in a plastic shopping bag with a broken handle. Campbell could remember the jeans but the sweater was new. He felt suddenly randy, and found he had quite run out of conventional small talk.

She looked at him as though she had sensed that too, then said, 'I'd better let you go and get on with finding out what you're supposed to be doing to help make Rosamund a professor.'

'Yes . . . I suppose so. . . . What are you doing on Friday evening?'

'You're not free. You're on for the ICU.'

'Christ. Yes. Oh. . . . Well. . . .'

'I'm going home on Saturday. How about . . .?'

'Friday morning? That's tomorrow.'

'Lovely.'

'Where are you and Bones?'

'Thirty-six Marchmont Terrace. Top left.'

'I'll be round about cock-crow. I'll bring some rolls.'

Campbell began to feel better: he had almost forgotten about his headache, and the numb, cotton-wool feeling in his throat and chest was starting to go away. He walked on in the sun, through the park and towards the Institute, not quite glad to be alive, but with the feeling that quite soon he might be. The black, restless hours between three and five in the morning, always the nadir of his toxic depression when he had drunk too much, and in this instance exacerbated by a confused infatuated longing for Jean in a variety of phantasmagoric guises, including the Virgin Mary, Astarte and Kali the Destroyer, now seemed far behind.

The park was green and ordinary, and at mid-morning almost deserted. A few toddlers, brightly coloured blobs in the distance, played in a little corral furnished with swings, a slide and a safe-looking municipal space ship. Some navvies had started to dig a trench and, having broached the tarmac of the walkway in a neat rectangle, were now leaning on their picks and shovels with the air of men who had all day to light their pipes. A mad lady walked past with her family of nine black dachshunds flopping and cavorting like a troupe of clockwork slugs. Only the Institute, sprawling for a quarter of a mile behind tall railings to the north, marred his morning view.

Campbell had often wondered what the Royal Charitable Institute would look like from the air; what (in his darker moments as a houseman) it would look like nestling neatly in the cross-hairs of a bomb-aimer's sight. It was a large, untidy hospital, packed into its perimeter like a mediaeval city. All the original buildings remained, stone-built pavilions, moored to connecting corridors like huge mastless three-decker Scottish baronial prison-hulks, decorated with turrets, corbels and crow-stepped gables.

Perhaps, as originally conceived, the hospital had once been blessed with open spaces where the cold winds of the capital might disperse the noxious influences of the pre-antibiotic era, but decade by decade since the turn of the century those spaces had been filled by motley additions reflecting the proliferation of medical and paramedical departments, an increasingly fierce struggle for survival in an environment of limited potential, and a decline of aesthetic and building standards.

The present-day Institute offered a visible record of all these trends, from the radiology department, solid and gracious in a prime site near the centre, to last year's cyto-genetics laboratory in its gimcrack instant hut poised for take-off from the flat roof of one of the original Victorian edifices. Intermediate essays in red-brick, rough-cast, concrete and glass, aluminium and glass and just glass, fitting together like the pieces of a jig-saw, filled all the remaining interstices except the coke dump, the car parks and the solitary lawn outside the coffee lounge.

A complete new Institute had been at the planning stage for years. It was still talked of but no longer hoped for. Old Creech mentioned it occasionally when he thought that everyone had had enough of Burma. He sat on the planning committee, as had his predecessor of twenty years before, and in one of his brighter moments had suggested sending the senior student on the unit along to a few of its meetings, as he was the person present most likely to be still practising medicine when the thing was actually built. But on the whole, discussions of the New Institute, like thoughts of the kingdom of heaven, had been relegated from the category of likelihood to that of consoling fantasy amid pressing present misery.

Earlier that morning, when Campbell had realised he was not going to arrive at work much before eleven o'clock, he had a few moments of anxiety. Rational analysis, however, had been reassuring: he had no stated duties on Thursday mornings, he was based in an office far from Rosamund's and therefore from detection by a superior, and anyone looking for him would, in that unlikely event, assume that he was in a lab or a library, or sitting in the observation gallery of an operating theatre, waiting for a little piece of someone. His tasks for the day were mainly the half dozen things he had meant to do the previous day, together with taking a quick look, in Jean's company, at his three female in-patients and doing

Creech's colitis clinic for Ratho in the afternoon. Apart from the last item, which occurred at a time fixed by someone else, he could plan things to his own convenience.

To a recently retired houseman, accustomed to being at the beck and call of a dozen doctors and three dozen patients for twenty-four hours a day, it came as an awesome realisation, almost as fundamental as being parted forever from the bleep to which his ear had become attuned, like a sheepdog's to his master's whistle, for over a year. He was his own boss. He strode on in the sun, filled with this new feeling of freedom. He could go out to the bank if he wanted to, when he wanted to. He could go to the medical bookshop and stop off for a haircut on the way back if he felt like it. He could do his heavier reading at home, undisturbed, and resolved there and then that if, by any chance, he happened to meet Rosamund shortly at the main gate, and she should make suspicious noises, he would indicate vaguely that he had started on that laudable practice already.

Despite these thoughts, he walked into the hospital feeling like a spy trying out a new false moustache, and was relieved to arrive in the research fellows' room without threat or mishap. The occupant of the desk in front of Roddy's, a girl from the year above, also in some sort of research post, was sitting knitting. He smiled at her as he hung up his jacket.

'I'm actually working,' she said.

'Oh.'

'I've got a patient doing the new thing for upper gut secretions. Bill's stuff.'

'That radioactive thing?'

'Yes. The scans have to be done every fifteen minutes.'

'I see. I suppose you can't really get on with anything else.'

'No. It works out at about seventeen rows a time, with time to walk along to the scanning lab.'

'Oh. How's it going?'

'Not too bad. I should finish this sleeve today.'

'No. I meant the scan thing.'

'I don't think it's as good as the thing we're comparing it with. The old PVPP thing. But we've got the machine and it won't do anything else, and the company's given us the money. So we really just have to get on with it.'

'Are you working for Bill?'

'I'm working *with* him,' she said with some emphasis. Campbell remembered the unit secretary's delphic remarks about Bill's 'distractions' and 'family problems', and wondered if he were looking at them. 'What are you doing?' she asked.

'The faecal vitamin thing.'

'I thought they were into faecal proteins.'

'They were, but the protein money ran out. Then some came up for the vitamin thing.'

'With Rosamund?'

'For Rosamund.'

Ratho came in, wearing his infuriating linen jacket. He took it off and put on his white coat. Campbell decided to have coffee upstairs instead of in the male ward as he had done yesterday.

'Hello, Dilys. Hello, David.'

'Hi, Fraser.'

'Hello.'

'Well, David, how's the research going?'

'Coming along quietly.'

'Good. . . . I hope you're remembering about Dr Creech's clinic this afternoon.'

'Yes.' Campbell noticed that this morning there was yellow paint on Ratho's hands and fingernails.

'There's one lady. . . . She's a bit . . . sort of special . . . if you know what I mean. A very nice lady. Dr Creech is fond of her too. . . . I thought I'd better just mention. . . .'

'What?'

'Well, she's a very nice lady, and we've been giving her slightly . . . special treatment.'

'Yes?'

'I remember as a resident you used to sometimes, when it was busy . . . be a little. . . .'

'Yes?'

'You know. Of course we all agree you're very . . . efficient. But you know what I mean.'

'What's her name?'

'Mrs Alexander. I'm sure you'll like her too. And please give her my personal regards and regrets about having been unable to do the clinic.'

'Okay.'

He went off to coffee: downstairs, Campbell hoped.

Dilys was smiling.

'If the bugger doesn't trust me with his nice patients, why the hell does he ask me to do his clinics?'

'Oh, you know Fraser. Pussyfooting around not offending anybody.'

'If I got offended,' said Campbell, 'I'd be offended.'

'But you're not.'

'No. But I'm wondering why I'm doing his clinic.'

'I was wondering the same thing last week.'

'Really?'

'It makes one wonder. Generally.'

'I was wondering why the colour of the paint on his hands keeps changing.'

'You have the makings of an observant clinician, young Campbell.'

'I wonder.'

After a pause Campbell asked her if she had been for coffee.

'Three more rows, a quick scan then I'm going upstairs.'

At medical school Dilys had had a reputation for unhurried efficiency: she had had a good time and passed her exams with distinction. It was obvious even from the way she knitted. Campbell sat down at his desk with the list of things he should have done the previous day, until she came back from the scanning room, then they went upstairs for coffee.

Jean was not there. Sister poured the coffee and offered round biscuits in the manner of the perfect but slightly threatening hostess, dispensing privileges that might well be withdrawn. The contrast with the proletarian cafeteria run by her colleague downstairs was too obvious for comment. Even Creech noticed it: when he had coffee upstairs he did not dip his biscuit in it.

Dilys left after a silent count of seventeen rows and Campbell did not linger. As he went out of the ward he glimpsed Jean at the far end of it, working among the grannies who just lived there, or perhaps simply chatting with them.

Thoughts of Jean and hence of the ward round and Mrs Herron triggered Campbell's conscience on the subject of

primary biliary cirrhosis and his proposed revision of it. He
went back to his desk for some paper then took one of the
less direct but more interesting routes through the hospital
and across to the university library, meeting no one of note
but picking up a *Telegraph* from the hospital shop on the
way.

The library was a pleasant place to spend half an hour: a
patina of studious calm enveloped Campbell as soon as he
passed through its silent doors on to its discreet thick deep-
blue carpet. He knew from experience that the improving glow
wore off and was succeeded by frank boredom in an average
of about forty-five minutes, but that was quite compatible
with both some light hepatic reading and a quick pre-lunch
ward round with Jean, if available. He chose a fat, wise-
looking book with 'liver' in its title and filled out a borrower's
slip, scribbling 'FVPS' in the space marked 'Unit or Department'.

As a second-rate cathedral might be at a similar hour of the
day, the library was thinly populated, similarly by a selection
of the most faithful and the most idle of the community. As
he chose a desk Campbell noted examples of both. There was
a girl who produced endless publications on mouse prosta-
glandins as though by a strange compulsion, and a senior clinician who as editor of one of Edinburgh's longest running text-
books saw his darling through edition after edition from year
to year, working at it continuously, like the painters on the
Forth Bridge. Perhaps its twenty-fifth edition in the not too
distant future would be celebrated by a suitable plaque above
the desk where he had laboured. A couple of Ph.D. sufferers sat
entrenched behind ramparts of open volumes, respectively
sucking a ballpoint pen and gazing up at the ceiling.

At twenty to twelve Jean was sitting at the desk in the duty
room with the case notes for Rosamund's patients in front
of her. For a moment Campbell wondered if they had arranged
a round at a specific time, then remembered that their joint
forward planning had consisted only of 'See you tomorrow'
said with telepathic simultaneity after their brush with Sister.
She was not as pretty as Campbell recalled or imagined or

whatever. Her off-white coat of yesterday had been exchanged for one representing the Institute laundry's highest standard of transfiguration radiance, but she was wearing the same blouse. That puzzled Campbell, who in the depths of bachelor self-neglect managed a shirt a day, even if it meant occasionally buying a new one he did not need. Maybe the rules were different for girls' blouses, or perhaps she had been up all night. The duty room had the same totally organised ready-for-inspection ambience, in which she sat calmly and possessively as if she were about to ask him to take a seat and be interviewed.

She did not, but got up, picked up the case notes and walked over to join him at the door. They had reached the ward before either spoke.

'Nothing much has happened to your lot really.'

'Good.' That was the appealing side of the physician's trade. Nothing much happened. The patients got slowly better or worse. Doctors intervened only after much discussion or self-communing, usually using things that worked slowly if at all, and if they weren't feeling as strenuous as that they did nothing, stood back and congratulated themselves on their masterly inactivity. There was also a minority school who wanted to do things; surgeons in physicians' clothing, of whom Bill Dempster, Campbell's predecessor, was possibly one. They were correspondingly dangerous but normally well-buffered by their more traditional colleagues' inertia. Campbell, who had reservations about killing people, saw his physicianly development in terms of informed conservatism, or inertia redeemed by insight.

There was little in the round on which to contemplate intervention, or even exercise judgement. Mrs Innes, who now claimed to be ninety-seven, was well; Theresa the mongol had just started on a ten-day stool collection for Phase One and Mrs Herron's prothrombin time, estimated on a sample of blood taken the previous day, indicated that her blood clotting mechanisms were still too feeble to permit a repeat of her liver biopsy. Campbell wondered what he would have done had it been otherwise.

They left the ward at a safe two minutes to twelve and found themselves in the duty room once more.

'Any problems?' asked Campbell, fairly confident that there weren't.

'Nothing much. Someone wants to see somebody about Theresa. Someone from St Cuthbert's.'

'A nun?'

'No. A monk. Or maybe a priest.'

'Problems?'

'Sort of. . . . They're wondering why she's still here.'

'Coming up today?'

'After lunch. Could you see him?'

'I suppose so. Hang on. What's actually happening to her?'

Jean made a puzzled/amused face and spread her hands out in a 'Don't ask me' sort of way.

'Well. What's she had?'

'Just about everything. Some twice.'

'Anything abnormal?'

'No. Well, nothing important.'

'Who's interested?'

'Bill. The first isotope thing was a bit abnormal so he wants to repeat it when he gets some more of the stuff.'

'When's that?'

'Maybe next week.'

'And meanwhile?'

'Another ten-day stool collection for Phase One. The vitamin thing.'

'Does Rosamund know?'

'Her idea.'

'I hope this guy isn't a Jesuit or anything.'

She laughed, and looked as pretty as he had thought her, then said, 'Oh, and there's another blood film back on Mrs Herron. It sounds odd.'

'What sort of things?'

'Her haemoglobin's not bad. Ten grams. But the film is all burr cells and elliptocytosis and mexican hat cells and things like that.'

'Oh. That just means funny-shaped red cells. They go that way because in cirrhosis they pick up extra cholesterol.'

'Do they?'

'It's associated with depressed levels of serum lecithin-cholesterol acyl-transferase activity.'

Her eyes widened. 'Is it? . . . Do you know an awful lot?' She paused and smiled then said, 'Or have you just been reading up on it?'

She was sitting on the edge of the desk swinging her legs a bit in a way that from almost anyone else would have been a signal as unambiguous as an army cook battering a dixie lid with a ladle and roaring 'Come and get it!' When she did it it was just sitting on the edge of a desk swinging her legs a bit. Campbell wondered if she had already driven hundreds of men mad without realising it. She pursed her lips then said, 'I suppose it's a bit early to go for lunch. But shall we anyway?'

Campbell was glad to be relieved of the burden of initiative but resolved to suggest lunch himself the next time the problem arose. Bearing in mind her precedent of physiological frankness he excused himself to go to the loo, in much the same terms as she had used. When he came back she had taken off her white coat.

'I'm taking my bleep to lunch today.'

'Sister might prefer it.'

Once more they sat in the quietest corner of the general mess and Campbell reflected that if he had observed other people behaving as they were behaving he might begin to think things about them. He also wondered how often you had to do something before it qualified as a habit.

'Are you feeling all right?'

'People keep asking that.'

'But are you?'

'Yes. But people treat people who've had hepatitis as if they'd come back from the dead.'

'I didn't mean that. . . . You're looking . . . a bit grey round the eyes. Didn't you sleep well?' The tone of her concern was exactly halfway between her bedside manner and the drowsy intimacy of their talking on the grass the previous afternoon.

'Partly that.'

'And that looks a bit like a gastric diet.' She pointed to his lunch of soup and yoghurt and her beautiful eyes went serious. Again her suspected alcohol-phobia came to mind. Or was she simply being over-concerned in a time-passing

light-conversational way. Campbell decided to take charge
and drive things back into her territory before she reduced
him to patient if not chronic-alcoholic status.

'It's just the thought of the stodge. One of the worst things
about being a houseman was the food.'

'I suppose so. Practically all the girls doing housejobs get
fat.'

'You're not. You don't even look tired.'

'Don't I?'

'You haven't got the look at all.'

'What look?'

'The female houseman look.'

'What's that?'

'Oh, you know. Greasy hair. Porridgey complexion. Yesterday's make-up because she practically didn't get to bed at
all, poor dear. Dr Scholl's sandals and walks like a collapsing
cab-horse.'

'I think I know what you mean.' She was smiling again. 'But
there's no need to be unkind. I sometimes wear my Scholls.'

'You'll get feet like an au pair girl. Or a camel.'

'Oh no I won't.'

'Wait and see.'

The damage, if any, was repaired and the rest of lunch passed
innocuously in sub-intimate badinage which would, in other
circumstances – at a party or meeting a friend of a friend in a
pub – have signified considerable mutual interest and indicated
a follow-up of some sort. In this case the nature of the follow-
up, like the location of the table they had lunched at, was
pre-determined: they would have gone for coffee even if he
had not suggested it. They were standing in the Institute's un-
failingly exasperating coffee queue when her bleep went off.

'Oh hell. An admission. I said I'd have an early lunch and
see her as soon as she came in. I'd forgotten all about it.' She
looked at him as though it were all very serious, then said,
'Sorry,' and after a pause, 'Oh. The monk.'

'The monk?'

'Theresa's monk.'

'Oh, him. Yes. When?'

'I said just after lunch. About a quarter to two.'

'Okay. I'll try and think of something to say.'

'Hello.' A large powerfully built girl with a cup of coffee slopping in its saucer advanced across the lawn to interrupt Campbell's glum reverie.

'Hello . . . ?'

'I'm Jo Smith.'

'Oh. . . . David Campbell.'

'I'm sorry I had to rush off yesterday morning. But thanks anyway.'

'For what?'

'The bit of breast.'

'Oh.'

'Yes. The theatre technician gave it to me. It was a good one. Makes our series almost statistically significant.'

'Oh. I'm glad.' Perhaps some theatre technician with an interest in the quiet life and a knowledge of the Smith's predatory requirements had done the decent thing independently. No further explanation was indicated.

'You should have been up there this morning.'

'Why?'

'Ainslie said you're interested in colon.'

'Yes.'

'There were two. A sigmoid carcinoma for partial colectomy and a double ureteric anastomosis. Would have been ideal for you. Especially the first one. You could have had miles of it.'

'Oh. I'm sorry I missed that.'

'Actually I nearly got a bit for you.'

'Did you?'

'But I didn't know what sort of fluid you wanted it in.'

'You shouldn't have bothered.'

'Honestly it would have been no trouble. In fact it's quite sensible to get bits for each other's work if we happen to be up there anyway. Don't you think so?'

'Yes. I'm sure it is.'

'If you want me to get things for you you've only got to tell me what you want and leave me some of your bottles. It's no trouble.'

'Well, thank you. . . . The method is still . . . in its early stages. When the thing's . . . running on a more regular basis . . . I'll certainly want all the specimens I can lay my hands on.'

'Oh. All right. Just let me know. . . . Is this your first project?' She sat down next to him on the garden bench, lifted her cup and emptied its saucer on the ground quite near Campbell's feet.

'Yes.'

'Mine too. Since I graduated anyway. I'm really caught up in it. It's . . . sort of exciting. Like exploring. Going somewhere no one else's been before. D'you feel that way? Is that what brought you into research?'

'That sort of thing.'

'And all the really good minds in medicine are in research. Everyone's so stimulating. Just being in the same room as the professor makes me *think*. Of course he pushes us all like mad too. We have to do a paper every week for his Friday seminar. He reads them all and the best one is the subject of the seminar.'

Even Rosamund hadn't stooped to that in her search for other people's ideas. Perhaps that was why she wasn't a professor yet.

'D'you do any clinical work?' said Campbell, casting around for a topic which would make less demands on his insincerity.

'No. The professor thinks that at my stage it's a distraction. I've done housejobs of course.' She had finished the unspilt portion of her coffee but did not appear to be in any hurry to go away. 'But he's encouraging me to think about sitting primary towards the end of next year.'

'Primary fellowship?'

'Yes.'

'You going in for surgery?'

She lifted her chin a little with an expression that looked like the beginning of one of her large-brain-on-short-fuse outbursts, familiar from the operating theatre observation gallery, but which faded quickly into mere acquiescence. He realised he had been half expecting her to shriek, 'Of course I am you nincompoop, d'you think I'd sit fellowship to be a postmistress?' but she was sweetness and light itself.

'The professor thinks not enough women stay in surgery.'

Her hair was greasy and her skin looked as if it was recovering only slowly from her housejobs. She talked for a quarter of an hour about herself and the thoughts of her professor, while Campbell thought about Jean. At half past one he excused himself, saying he had to go and see a priest. Her expression reflected puzzlement and possibly militant atheism on the brink of a scathing attack, but softened when he explained.

'Bye,' she said. 'Perhaps I'll see you tomorrow.'

'Yes. Perhaps.'

The priest was small and fat, with dark green nylon socks and smelly feet. He offered Campbell a cigarette.

'No? Not while you're on duty, eh? Well take one for after.'

'No thanks. . . . I gather you wanted to talk to someone about Theresa.'

'That's right. I wondered if I might have a word. . . . You're sort of young to be a consultant.'

'Oh, I'm not a consultant. I'm just . . . supervising her care. Dr Fyvie's the consultant.'

'Is he around just now?'

'She.'

'What?'

'Dr Rosamund Fyvie. She's a lady. A lady doctor.'

'Oh I see. But you're not a consultant.'

Campbell was beginning to think about calling him 'your grace' by way of reprisal. 'No. But if there's anything I can help with. Any questions I perhaps could answer. I'd be only too glad.'

'I came up to see the consultant really. Is she not somewhere around?'

'She's not really expected on the ward this afternoon. Did you have an appointment with her?'

'The young doctor, whatever she's called, said I would see someone in charge.'

'Well, I'm sort of in charge. What was it you wanted to discuss?'

'Well . . . doctor. Over at St Cuthbert's we're caring sort of people. We reckon Theresa's place is with us. It's her home in fact. Her own home being for various reasons never really

a going concern. . . . In fact her father. . . . But that's by
the way. We give her a home, and she's happy there.'

'Yes?'

'And we think she should be back with us.'

'Of course. So she will be.'

'Ah, but the question is when, doctor?'

'Quite.'

'Well?'

'Yes.' Campbell was painfully aware of his lack of conviction
in any argument to retain his consultant's patient, and was
annoyed to find himself beginning to sound like his adversary.
'There's a certain amount of . . . uncertainty about that.'

'So there would seem to be. What's the matter with her?'

Campbell lacked the courage to say 'Nothing'. So he said,
'There are one or two tests still to be done. And some results
we're still waiting for.'

'Is she any better than she was?'

'I think we could probably say that she is.'

'Most certainly. Her whole condition has improved entirely,
according to some who've seen her daily for coming on three
weeks.'

'So I gather.'

'You gather, doctor?' Campbell wondered if the man spent
his spare time watching courtroom dramas on the mother
superior's television.

'Well I've just . . . taken over her management from the
last chap. Not that that makes any difference of course.'

The priest smiled like a sporting and generous victor at the
card table. 'You feel as I do myself, doctor.' He chuckled,
showing filthy yellow teeth separated by thick greenish lines.
'Shall we say tomorrow, doctor? The way the nuns are missing her is cruelty itself to watch. And there's another poor
wee mongol creature, Dolores. . . . You should see them together.'

The door behind Campbell opened and the priest got up.
Campbell turned round to see Rosamund Fyvie, his clinical
mentor and research supervisor, bearing down on him.

'Ah, Dr Campbell.'

Campbell got up too. 'Dr Fyvie, this is Father . . .'

'Herdman. Aloysius Herdman.'

'Father Herdman. So glad you could come. I've been wanting to talk to you. So glad I've caught you at last.' She indicated by a courtly gesture that he should be seated and took Campbell's seat herself.

'That's two of us. It's about wee Theresa.'

'Of course. We've all been very concerned about her.'

'Concerned? I thought she was getting better.'

'She's looking better.'

'Looking better?'

'Yes.'

'Is there something sort of . . . going on?'

'We're doing our best to find out.' She composed her face in a mask of pre-Raphaelite wisdom, sincerity and concern, which was quite a feat considering she was all of forty and on the big side too. Campbell remembered how he had been persuaded to apply for his present post in the first place. 'It hasn't been at all easy. . . . Her original symptoms I'm glad to say have partially receded, but a lot of important questions remain unanswered. And of course it's all just that bit more difficult against the background of . . . of. . . .'

'You mean what with her being a mongol?'

Beatific joy joined the other pre-Raphaelite expressions on Rosamund's face. 'I knew you'd understand.'

The priest smiled modestly. Rosamund went on. 'There's also the especially difficult question of evaluating her response to therapy.'

'What?'

'You see, Father Herdman, there are unique problems. Things that the ordinary run of the mill techniques like fibreoptic endoscopy might miss.'

'Quite,' said the priest.

Rosamund smiled again. 'So it becomes almost mandatory to move just a little closer to the advancing edge of scientific knowledge. For her benefit of course.'

'Of course.'

'So we've gone a little further than is usually necessary, with a technique that's being used for the first time this side of the Atlantic. But little Theresa won't be the only one to benefit.'

'You mean a sort of experiment?'

'No, no. Not an experiment. An evaluation. From which

others will benefit too.'

Peasant caution still lurked around the corners of his eyes. 'Is it a breakthrough?'

'We think it's a very significant advance. It's certainly helped a lot in her case . . .' The priest's eyebrows went up and he opened his mouth as though to speak, but Rosamund went on, '. . . already. And we're only halfway through the various procedures.'

'But will it be a benefit to others? As well as her.'

'Of course.'

'Oh well. I suppose that's nice.'

'Yes.' Rosamund smiled again.

'What with her being a mongol. It's nice she can help. She can't do much for her fellow creatures.'

'She can do a very great deal, Father Herdman. She's done a great deal already. And we'll keep you very closely informed about her further progress. Would it be too much trouble if I were to keep in touch with you personally by phone at St Cuthbert's?'

'Not at all.'

'Thank you very much for coming.'

The priest left, casting a disdainful glance at Campbell. As Rosamund and Campbell walked out of the visitors' room she remarked to him. 'Perhaps I should have mentioned it to him, I'm hoping Theresa will co-operate in the KM 1103 trial too.'

Without consciously trying to, Campbell had succeeded in evading Rosamund since their inaugural meeting early the previous day. On the research front he had little to report, or even ask about, nor had anything arisen from his clinical responsibilities to merit a consultant opinion. He thanked her for the list of references, which he said he found interesting, managing to leave it unclear as to whether he was talking about the list or the references themselves. She disappeared towards her office and Campbell went downstairs in good time to take Creech's Thursday colitis clinic on Ratho's behalf.

The first patient needed fewer tablets, the second more and the third was Dr Ratho's awfully nice lady who had been having slightly special treatment. She was a married woman in her early forties, tanned and in a careful state of preservation. She looked just a little bit unwell, though less so than the taciturn bus-conductor and the equally phlegmatic office-cleaner who had preceded her in the clinic.

'Has there been some mistake? I was expecting to see Dr Ratho.'

'Dr Ratho is unfortunately not able to do the clinic this afternoon. He asked me to give you his special apologies.'

'Oh. Will he be off long?'

'I shouldn't think so.'

'I could re-book my appointment.'

'You could.'

'Or I could just see you.'

'You could.' As a rule Campbell never found his personal reactions obtruding very much into his clinical encounters, but was aware that this one might involve a little self-control. Her face registered her decision by a sort of power surge of social charm.

'And what's your name?'

'Dr Campbell.'

'I don't think I've heard Dr Ratho talk of you. You weren't on the ward last time I was in, were you?'

'When was that?'

'It's all in my case notes, of course. I think the last time was about May. I have a chronic condition.'

'I see. How's it been lately?'

'Oh, just going along, much like always. Maybe a little worse than usual, if anything.'

'Blood?'

'A little.'

'Slime?'

'Not much.'

'Often?'

'Four or five times a day.'

'Any particular time?'

'Mainly mornings.'

'And how are you feeling generally?'

'I was hoping Dr Ratho was going to ask that.'

'Oh?'

'He thinks it's emotionally triggered. And he's so understanding.'

'Anything in particular?'

'Well, there is something. . . . My husband. . . . If he's not away, he's coming back, if you see what I mean.'

'Not really. Sorry.'

'He's at sea. Royal Fleet Auxiliary, actually.' She sounded as if she wanted to make it very clear that he didn't drive the corporation sludge boat from Leith. 'And he's always . . . coming . . . and going.' For a misguided moment Campbell wondered if he were about to have a tiresome conversation about premature ejaculation on Dr Ratho's behalf. But no. 'It's unsettling.'

'Related to your symptoms?'

'I wanted to discuss that with Dr Ratho.'

'Do you go abroad yourself?'

'Sometimes. I can join him on homeward trips. About twice a year usually.'

Campbell nodded to the nurse and said to the patient, 'May I examine your abdomen?'

She undressed quickly and sprang up on to the couch as though keen to show how far her tan went. She was wearing a bra and pants set of the expecting-to-be-seen bikini-like variety. There was a great deal of tan and midline scar below the umbilicus.

'I've had my womb out.'

Campbell glanced nervously at the nurse, who was having a quiet smile. There was no abdominal abnormality to feel. He took a blood sample from her arm and told her to get dressed, then went to his desk and started to read back into her notes. She had not been sigmoidoscoped for some time.

'Could you come back next week ready for a look inside. Monday at two in the afternoon. The nurse will give you instructions and some tablets to clear you out.'

'You mean look inside my bottom.' She made a face. 'Dr Ratho doesn't do that.'

'It's time someone did,' said Campbell gruffly.

'Ooh, you are horrid,' she said, making another tanned wrinkled grimace. 'What about my tablets?'

Campbell paused in physicianly thought. 'Take two more a day. And please make an appointment for next week.'

'Will it be Dr Ratho?'

'I expect so.'

'D'you think he'll do me?'
'It would be best to come prepared.'

When Campbell went upstairs for afternoon tea Bill Dempster was sitting alone with Jean in Sister's room, describing
a game of squash. He interrupted himself to say 'Hi Dave,'
and took the last egg sandwich. Campbell had some tea and
a ginger snap.

'You know what Bertram's like. Comes the cripple something
terrible. Tells you what a helluva hangover he's got and how
he was up all night with the wean's teeth. And then gets
cramp walking downstairs to the court. And keeps moaning
about being on the wrong side of thirty. So anyway we
warmed up and started and he kept getting to things I never
thought he'd get near and he was just keeping a bit ahead.
Then he really did get cramp. He was jumping up and down
on one leg saying, "Oh oh oh, it's bound to be a major deep
vein thrombosis. I'll get a pulmonary embolus and die. I'll
never drink again if I live. Oh I wish I'd said goodbye to
the bairn and the wife properly this morning." He got so
carried away with himself that when we started again I
grabbed a couple of quick points and won.'

Jean smiled at him, instead of emptying her tea-leaves over
his head, as Campbell would have preferred.

'So Jim had better be fit,' said Dempster, getting up. 'Must
go. Sorry, Dave. Helluva busy.'

'One admires his enthusiasm,' said Campbell after he had
gone.

'Yes,' said Jean, who was perhaps too nice to notice sar-
casm. 'Did Rosamund find you?'

'She did. It was a little bit nasty.'

'What was?'

'With her and that priest bloke. I got rather landed in it.'

'Oooh, yes. Sorry. It just sort of happened. She asked if I
knew where you were, then when I said, she said something
about feeling Theresa ought to be in for a little longer and
she'd see Bill about it. What did she want you for?'

'I don't think anything in particular. Maybe she was just
doing a spot check on everyone who's supposed to be helping
make her a professor. . . . What's KM 1103?'

'It's another of Bill's things. When he's being enthusiastic he says it'll put the surgeons right out of the ulcer business.'

'Any problems with my lot?'

'Only the priest.'

'He looked happy enough when I last saw him.'

'Oh?'

'Rosamund. Treated him like he was the pope.'

'She's very good with people.'

Campbell began to wonder if his assessment of this girl was premature: if she couldn't see that Dempster was a dilettante con-man and Rosamund a raging psychopath on the make, she couldn't be all that sharp. Or perhaps it was something to do with being reared in an alien tradition of medicine in the far north.

'Sometimes,' he grunted.

'That's what worries me. And Bill. His enthusiasm for things is sort of sometimes too. He's come unstuck with Rosamund once or twice.'

'Really?'

'It's not very nice of me to tell you, I suppose. But one day he muttered something about it being time he did some really solid reading, and spending a whole day in the library. Two days later he came back with a sunburned nose and couldn't resist telling me at tea how he'd just missed a lovely twelve pounder with a hand-tied Boston Strangler or something. And one of his waders leaking. Helluva lot of line screeching off his reel when Rosamund came in.' She was laughing in a way that made Campbell feel shivery all over.

'Has he been putting all my patients on that KM stuff?'

'I shouldn't think so. It only came this morning.'

She was sitting back, leaning a bit to one side, with her legs straight out in front of her. The fingers of her right hand lay loosely round the narrow wooden arm of the chair and in her left hand she held a biscuit. She started to eat the biscuit and Campbell wondered whether everything she did was done with that grace and ease and naturalness which had so captured him, or whether it was simply that he had been reduced to a state in which whatever she did seemed thus to him. He tried to imagine her doing something clumsy, like spilling tea on her skirt, or inelegant, like picking her nose, but couldn't. She leant back a little more and her breasts, not very large or firm or any special shape, but hers and beautiful, lifted the red and white pattern of her blouse. Rapidly and involuntarily, Campbell found himself imagining her doing a series of very interesting things, some of them more elegant than others, and culminating in a contained, grateful and ladylike orgasm, but all done with her own wry, gentle simplicity. He finished his tea, put his cup down and sat far back in his chair. She shifted her feet a little and her knees moved a further inch or so apart. This caused Campbell to catch his breath, while having to maintain, by a heroic effort of will, a facial expression appropriate to having tea with the married resident in Sister's room on a Thursday afternoon. She continued to eat her biscuit and eventually Campbell began to breathe again.

'Are you feeling all right?' She was looking at him with deep, grey-blue concern.

'Yes,' he said, smiling wanly. 'I keep having to tell people that.'

'But they say that about hepatitis. The feeling hangs around. You can sometimes feel lousy for months after the jaundice goes away.'

'So they say.'

'And it's worse if you drink.'

'Maybe if I joined the Band of Hope. . . .'

She laughed and said, 'I didn't mean it like that. . . . Have some more tea.' In pouring it she leaned forward towards him so that the top of her head came quite close, and Campbell's libidinous imaginings took charge again. She seemed to be almost but not quite aware of this, and almost but not quite discouraging.

Much as he would have liked to find out, Campbell did not feel that this was yet the sort of thing they could discuss directly. However, it was very easy just to be with her. He drank his tea and thought how relaxed and accessible they were towards each other: after a total of only a few hours together they appeared to have developed between them a knack of companionable silence and an awareness of each other's conversational and non-verbal cues that could be explained only by a very high degree of mutual interest. Campbell considered the implications of this in some detail until the appearance of a sinister pattern of tea-leaves prompted him to speculate that perhaps she simply had the dangerous gift of making everyone feel that way.

'David.'

'What?' Campbell wondered if she were as aware as he was that she had just used his Christian name for the first time.

'David. . . . D'you mind if we have a think about Mrs Herron?'

'Herron. Cirrhosis.'

'Yes. Mrs Herron. There are problems. . . .'

'Prothrombin time?'

'That as well, but really I meant the other things. You know. . . . Social. Her husband. He's talking about booking a holiday for when she gets out and all that sort of thing.'

'I see. Someone should talk to him.'

She leant forward again, and Campbell noticed a mannerism that he had half-noticed before: when she was being very serious about something her left eyebrow came down a little. 'I have already,' she said. 'He doesn't seem to take it in.'

'That's one way of coping.'

'Is it?'

'It'll do for now. She'll take a while. There were some kids too, weren't there? How are they?'

'You can see her trying to look well when they're there.'

'Good for her.'

'I like her.'

'Does she know she's booked?'

'I think so. But she pretends not to.'

'That's her way of coping.'

'You think people just cope?'

'I think they do. Not always in ways that make sense to the graduate mind.'

'That sounds awful.'

'It's true.'

By now it was uncomfortably late to be still sitting in Sister's room round a cooling teapot, even if one was discussing work. By tacit consent they got up and drifted along towards the duty room and stopped outside its door. Jean said, 'I'm still

worried about her.' They went into the duty room. She sa
down at her ever-tidy desk and Campbell sat opposite, stretch
ing his legs under it.

'Has she got God?' Campbell asked.

'What?' said Jean.

'Religion. Is she holy?'

'I don't know. I haven't asked her.'

'I couldn't,' said Campbell.

'Couldn't what?'

'Ask her about that. Not without sounding as if I was
measuring her for a box. "Good morning, Mrs Herron, I'd
just like to check that you've made your reservation under the
Sky Wise Pie Plan for a guaranteed trouble-free departure." '

Jean was laughing, but clearly also somewhat aghast. 'Are
you dead against religion?'

'Just not for it. You?'

She looked so beautiful and thoughtful that Campbell hoped
she would take minutes or hours to determine the state of
her soul. After a while she said quietly and with a touching
determination, 'We're for it. Jim and I.'

'Oh.'

'It makes marriage stronger.'

Campbell was beginning to wish he had not trodden on God
in the first place. A certain distance had been created. As the
conversation could not be erased, he took it further.

'Meaning you've got God as well as each other.'

To his surprise she took that seriously, and said, 'Yes,' with
an even more beautiful earnestness. Campbell smiled to em-
phasise his insincerity.

'And when one of you croaks the other one's still got God?'

She giggled nervously then smiled too. 'That's the idea. . . .
Sometimes I think you're just as horrible as you pretend you
are, Doctor Campbell. But I'll pray for you.'

'Thanks.'

'We both will.'

The mystery of holy matrimony deepened, but rather than
explore the determinants of singular and plural first person
pronoun usage by young marrieds, Campbell asked if Mrs
Herron and her relatives had been seen by the ward social
worker. They hadn't, and the houseman was instructed that

the omission should be rectified.

Despite their religious differences, neither Campbell nor Jean seemed in a hurry to terminate the conversation. She had the night off from five o'clock and with characteristic efficiency had finished her ward work hours ago; and Campbell, if truth were told, had nothing to do that he either wanted to do or had to do urgently, which in his particular case was almost the same as having nothing to do. They talked about Mrs Innes and her faithful visitors, the coalmen grandsons, and about Theresa and her protector who had made things awkward with Rosamund earlier in the afternoon, and of Rosamund herself.

It emerged that Jean's experience of her had been not unlike Campbell's.

'When I came down for the interview she was there with Dr Creech and Dr Kyle, and she really was nice to me. In fact I think it was because of her I got the job here. And afterwards when it was offered she wrote congratulating me and saying how nice it would be to have me working here. And . . . it wasn't just things like that, but the women in medicine thing generally. She's a consultant physician in a teaching hospital, and that's really quite something for a woman in medicine. The trouble is they sort of . . .'

'Get like the men? The men who are consultants in teaching hospitals?'

'I was going to say they get like the worst of the men. Nastily ambitious. A bit devious. . . . But there are other things about her. She's not married but she's not bitter and twisted about it either.'

'She's got her dogs and horses.'

'But she's not just the horsey type.'

'You know what people say.' What Bertram usually said was that she was sometimes bearable on Mondays if she'd spent all of Sunday with three-quarters of a ton of throbbing horsemeat between her thighs.

'That's silly. Hundreds of girls have a horsey stage and some of them keep it up. I did, and I would keep it up if we could afford it.'

'It's the way she treats people that worries me.'

'People or patients?' said Jean.

'What?'

She smiled ruefully. 'You know what I mean. People meaning people like us. Or the patients.'

'Meaning people like Theresa. I don't think she makes a distinction. We're all in the business of helping to make her a professor. People and patients.' Campbell smiled like a wicked uncle. 'And that, my dear children, is the meaning of medical research.'

Jean made a face and said, 'And what are you doing in it? Do you want to be a professor in the nineteen nineties?'

'I don't think I do. I can't make up my mind whether it's because I'm not nasty enough or because I don't care enough.'

'Maybe it's because you're not clever enough.'

'That might be it.'

'Then what are you doing in research?'

'I don't know. It's expected behaviour, I suppose. I did clever housejobs and didn't have anything lined-up for afterwards and things happened and I got asked, by our accomplished and persuasive gauleiter Rosamund, as it happens, to come and do this.'

'Regrets?'

'Come on. I've only been in research two days. But I might add my tuppenceworth to the sum of human knowledge.'

'Knowledge of faecal vitamins?' she enquired, with malicious innocence.

Campbell wondered if Jim the frog enthusiast got a lot of this sort of thing over the cornflakes at home. He defended his present employment.

'After a preliminary survey of the literature I am now in a position from which I may eventually advance to prove conclusively that faecal vitamins have nothing to do with anything. In particular with colitis, diverticulitis, cancer, halitosis and ingrown toenails.' Jean was laughing again. 'It may be a lifetime's work, but already it's becoming clearer. I could start by proving they had nothing to do with a few important things. Then get some Ph.D. students to tidy up the odd little corners, like "Bantu diet as reflected in faecal vitamins" and "Faecal vitamins in albino coypus". My epidemiological group would do prospective cohort studies on how faecal vitamin assay is of no use in predicting who's going to get appendicitis. And my clinical staff would devote themselves to proving that vitamins had nothing to do with any known form of cancer. You've got to be in cancer. That's where the big money is.'

Jean was wriggling in her chair with amusement. 'The David Campbell Faecal Vitamin Research Institute.'

'They can't call it that till I've retired, laden with years and glory.'

'The Sir David Campbell Faecal Vitamin Research Institute.'

'That's better. D'you want to join?'

'Sounds super. But we wouldn't do mongols.'

'No. No mongols. By order of the management.'

Unnoticed amid their amusement and their brief absorption with each other Sister had come quietly into the duty room.

'Dr Campbell?'

'Yes, Sister.'

She was looking at him in what Bertram called her small-mouthed way. Perhaps she had overheard his last remark out of context.

'Dr Campbell. A doctor on the phone for you. I didn't catch his name. Bar something.'

'Thanks, Sister.'

It was Bones, with whom he shared a flat, ringing up to ask Campbell if he had thought about what they were going to eat that evening and how about a pint at five anyway. When he went back to the duty room Jean was still there. They talked until about five to five, then Campbell asked her if she would like to join him and Bones for a drink across the road. She said she would have liked to, but couldn't that evening because it was her turn to cook. They left the ward together.

'See you tomorrow.'

'See you tomorrow.'

Campbell met Bones at five. They stayed in the pub until it closed at ten, dining from a selection of crisps and peanuts, and drinking a great deal.

'Hello.'

'Hello. . . . You look terrible.'

'Oh. The usual reasons. Come in.'

'I've brought some rolls.'

'Good. Come in here. Nowhere else is respectable.'

They went into the kitchen, which wasn't particularly respectable either. Things that Campbell had not noticed when just he and Bones were around became more apparent. There was a heap of unwashed plates of uncertain age standing to the right of the sink, and some bread that was beyond eating but not quite ready for throwing out sitting for some reason on an old *Lancet* on the table.

'David, you're beginning to get squalid.'

'D'you think so?' Campbell filled up the kettle for coffee. 'How was Intensive Care?'

'Not too bad. . . . Sit down. You look awful.'

'Okay.' Campbell sat down on a kitchen chair. He was still in his dressing gown, and had not shaved and felt almost but not quite as bad as he had done the previous morning.

'Are you making a habit of getting drunk?'

'Twice isn't a habit. Just bad luck. Or bad company.'

'Bones?'

'Yes.'

'Is he still alive?'

'I think so. He left at seven, poor bugger.'

'What for?'

'Thoracic theatre. I don't know how they can stand it. Peering into big holes in people's chests before breakfast time.'

'I hear you had a good session.'

'Oh?'

'One of the girls went across for a quick one before coming on night duty.'

'Oh. We just went for a five o'clock pint and couldn't decide where to eat before it was too late.'

'Anyone interesting there?'

'Not really.'

The kettle boiled and Campbell started to get up.

'Sit down,' said Joan. 'I'll get it.' She made two cups of coffee. 'Have you got anything to cook for breakfast?'

'No.' There wasn't anything and even if there had been he would not have wanted it. 'Sorry. Are you very hungry?'

'Not very. Have a roll.'

'Thanks.'

'Got any marmalade?'

'Bones' mother sends us about a ton a month. It's in that cupboard.'

Campbell sat watching Joan cutting and buttering the rolls. She was wearing jeans and a big floppy jersey under which, he knew from experience, it was probable that she was wearing nothing else. He rearranged his dressing gown, and tied the cord more firmly.

'How's the flat working out?' she asked. 'Apart from the squalor.'

'Not bad. It's somewhere to lay my weary head and keep my LPs and my paperbacks out of the rain.'

'How's Bones?'

'Oh, much the same. Never a dull moment. He went home last weekend and brought back his train set.'

'What?'

'Toy trains. There's a depot in his bedroom, a big loop round the lounge sofa and a siding out into the bathroom. He says it helps him relax.'

'Relax from what?'

'The stress of killing people up in thoracic, I suppose. And he's doing primary.'

'Fellowship?'

'Wants to be a surgeon when he grows up. But meantime he lies on the floor with a Hornby Dublo GWR Pacific in pieces on the carpet and a Cunninghame's Anatomy open in front of him in case anyone comes in.'

'What about you?'

'I never was one for toy trains.'

'I meant higher qualifications.'

'I thought you did.'

'Are you going to do membership and be a proper physician?'

'I suppose so.'

'When?'

'In due course.'

'How's the research going?'

'I'm beginning not to believe in it. But I'll have to start something soon. Rosamund expects that every man will do his duty.'

'How's the clinical stuff?'

'I like that.' Campbell was about to enthuse over the junior staff when he realised it would be scarcely appropriate in the circumstances. 'It's quite nice to be back in the unit. Everybody's still the same, and a few things have happened but nothing much has changed. Like missing a few months of the Archers. Walter Gabriel Creech just goes on and on.'

'He's sweet.'

'The more I find out about Rosamund the more I appreciate his outstanding quality of benign inertia.'

'That sounds like his obituary for the BMJ.'

'I suppose it does. "D.C. writes: The variety and unsurpassed kindness of the ways Henry Creech found of doing nothing never ceased to amaze his wide circle of friends. He will be sorely missed." '

Joan was sitting near Campbell, on the same side of the table, eating her roll and drinking coffee. Looking at her, he began to remember an awful lot of things about her. Not just obvious things he could see, like her large capable nursey hands and her hairstyle, which had in any case changed to a shorter, easy-to-look-after cut, but silly things like the way she cleaned her teeth (textbook up-and-down) and what her ears tasted like. She half-turned to look out of the window and he remembered her shoulders and how they felt to sleep against, and how the smell of her skin changed gradually through the night, from soapy, straight from the shower, to a subtler warmer totally characteristic smell of her own that came on slowly over about six hours. She turned towards him again and was looking at him expectantly.

'Well, Doctor Campbell?'

'Well what?'

'I was wondering if you'd like some more coffee.'

From a familiar and welcome expression on her face it was obvious that whatever they said or did by way of preliminaries – the word courtship was far too formal – they would be in bed together within five minutes.

'Before?' he asked.

'If you feel you must.'

She got up and came very much closer.

'Come here.'

She stood astride his legs, holding his head against her. Campbell put his arms round her waist, and remembered the weight and resilience of her hips. He pushed up her sweater and nuzzled her midriff, while she ran her fingers through his hair. He found her navel with his tongue and licked it and then blew sharply in it.

'Ooooh,' she said. 'I can feel that right inside me.' She backed off him and pulled her chair up and sat facing him, with her knees outside his. Her eyes were soft with lust. She slid a hand under his dressing gown.

'Mmmmm. I thought you were sitting a little awkwardly.'

They lingered for a moment over moist, tonguing kisses then she stood up again.

'I suppose you've got a squalid bed somewhere.'

Campbell walked over to the Institute just after half past eleven, feeling at peace with the world. While Joan slept on in his bed, with an alarm clock set for four o'clock ticking away beside her, he faced his day's work with that calm self-assurance that only successful lovers know. The minor eccentricity of a morning session only added to his sense of well-being: while the vast majority of the sexually active population had been typing or driving or daydreaming or looking down holes in chests or dozing on physicianly ward rounds or whatever they happened to do for a living, he and Joan had revelled in the delights of fleshly reconciliation. The little games and habits of their physical familiarity, not lost but sharpened by their not having slept together for more than six months, left a tingling glow that kept him musing happily all the way across the park.

It was not love, he decided, but it was more than just randy nostalgia. They liked each other, and sex together was marvellous. Or did they like each other *because* sex was marvellous? Campbell contemplated that question as he walked past the labourers digging up the footpath. One man, standing in a knee-deep hole and tapping delicately at its edge with a pick, seemed to read his thoughts, giving him a broad smile and a dirty wink. In return Campbell bade him a courteous good morning.

Even the Institute took on a less malign aspect: its clutter of little spires offering, on that felicitous morning, the suggestion of a fairy-tale town rather than the usual aura of grim custody. He entered its gates with a sense of anticipation, and breathed the first of its complex pattern of odours with a connoisseur's pleasurable recognition.

When he got to the ward Jean was sitting at her desk in the duty room, looking more beautiful than ever. She was writing in a file of case notes which Campbell recognised as Mrs Herron's.

'Hello.'

'Hello, David.'

'Everybody all right?'

She said, 'I think so,' adding, 'All three of them.'

'Good. I just wanted to check on a few things.'

'Oh?'

'For Rosamund's Friday round.'

'Yes.' Jean was smiling, perhaps patronisingly. A suspicion clouded Campbell's euphoria. 'When does she go round . . . this afternoon?'

'She doesn't,' said Jean, smiling very broadly now. 'She goes round in the morning.'

'Oh.'

'An hour ago.' She was laughing.

'I see. That's awkward.'

'Yes.'

'Creates a bad impression.'

'It might.'

'First consultant ward round.'

'Yes.'

Campbell was silent. Jean said, 'I shouldn't worry.'

'Oh?'

'No. I said you hadn't been looking at all well yesterday.'

'Thanks.'

'You got discussed over coffee.'

'Did I?'

'Yes. Creech was there. He said he'd noticed you weren't

looking quite right and thought you might have been sickening for something.'

'That was nice of him.'

'It ended up with everyone sort of agreeing it was brave of you to be working at all, having been so ill. Even Rosamund.'

'Really? . . . Oh. . . . I suppose that means I'd better go away and just get on with being ill. Before anyone else sees me.'

'Might be best.' She looked at him for a moment then said, 'Don't fret. Bill used to do things like that too.'

'With all his commitments?'

'Yes.'

She got up and gathered the case notes in her arms, and came over towards him. Campbell remembered how much he cared about her. Standing very close to him, holding the case notes against herself like a breastplate of righteousness, she looked earnestly into his eyes and said, 'Oh, David.'

'What?'

'Sometimes I worry about you.'

Campbell left the ward and, succumbing suddenly to a good resolution, went across to the library and looked out one or two references on the faecal vitamin pilot study. After half an hour it occurred to him that it might be awkward to be seen there if he were officially off sick. He was, moreover, bored. He remembered that Joan was still at the flat, went back there and after some deliberation woke her. She was pleased to see him and they stayed happily in bed together, rediscovering familiar ecstasies, until the alarm went off at four, and even after.

At two minutes past six the man who organised the rota for night cover of the intensive care unit was standing anxiously at the unit's door. He smiled at Campbell but his smile faded as Campbell came nearer.

'Are you sure you're all right for tonight? I heard you'd been off earlier today.'

'I'll manage.'

'You sure?'

'I think so.'

'You don't look at all well.'

The limited number of variations on this recurrent theme were all beginning to grate on Campbell, who knew he looked horrible. A glance in a mirror before leaving the flat had confirmed the combined ravages of a hangover and a day at the sex Olympics with Joan, who at times in the afternoon had appeared to be not so much recapturing the joys of the previous October as attempting to catch up on all the lost joys in between.

'I feel okay.'

'Good. I was half resigned to staying on and doing the night myself. It's great you can do it. Shall we go round?'

The intensive care unit consisted of a converted ward in which an arc of eight cubicles was arranged round a central control desk laden with a formidable amount of whirring, buzzing and flashing gadgetry. For each cubicle there was a vertical bank of monitoring equipment giving continuous readings of pulse rate, electrocardiogram and sundry other variables concerned with precarious survival in the electronic age. Two staff nurses sat at the desk looking remarkably unworried; looking indeed as though they would have been equally happy supervising a battery of intercontinental ballistic missiles or a busy afternoon's air traffic control at Heathrow. As he passed them Campbell noted that one of them had a screwdriver and a small pair of pliers in her top pocket.

The ICU man waved airily at the console. 'Don't worry about that. They know it all. Your job's mainly clinical. Admitting new patients. Helping with resuscitation. Getting in any specialists you need. Writing up the drugs. Oh . . . and certifying the deaths of course.'

'I see.'

'It's been quiet all week.'

'Good.'

'So you've got three empty beds to play with.'

They stopped in front of the first occupied cubicle. 'This chap's probably okay. He had a twinge of chest pain and got a bit anxious. His GP was worried too and the medical registrar wasn't sure so he's in here just to be on the safe side. Frankly it sounds like indigestion but one doesn't want to go putting it in writing. It creates certain problems and of course if you do that sort of thing the results begin to suffer.'

'The results?'

'The coronary survival results.'

'Oh. Okay. Are you giving him antacids?'

'No. . . . It looks bad on an intensive care unit.'

'Okay.'

'And this chap. . . .'

A loud high-pitched buzz came from the region of the desk and a bright red light flashed on and off, theatrically illuminating the down-turned faces of the two nurses. One leant over the offending machine and fiddled with its controls. They muttered quietly together and the screwdriver changed hands. From inside the cubicle next to Campbell came a long, full-throated groan.

'I think it's this chap,' said the ICU man.

'Hang on,' said one of the nurses.

'Coming,' said the other.

'Probably both of you would be best,' said the ICU man. Both nurses walked quickly into the cubicle.

'Do we go in too?' Campbell asked.

'Best to give them a couple of minutes. Otherwise they get offended. . . . The next one. . . .'

Campbell was not listening to his guide. The sounds from within the cubicle were much more engrossing: the firm thump over the heart, the recurrent thud of the chest being compressed to maintain blood flow, the sigh of air in the ventilating tube. He remembered with a sickening shock the last time he had heard such noises.

His guide droned on. 'So she's a possible infero-lateral, with no conduction problems so far and we would probably pace her if she got any but I'm not so sure since she's already had a stroke with a total right-sided paralysis and loss of speech. . . . But she's okay from the cardiac point of view.'

Campbell had not thought of Mac's death for some time, and to be reminded of it thus brought it back with a directness and sudden impact that shocked him all over again. The noises were those he had heard from the next cubicle when he had been lying, very ill himself, in the Institute's isolation unit only eight months previously. For a deranged moment Campbell wondered whether if he were to open the door of the curtained cubicle, Mac would be lying there yellow and inert, with tubes and leads everywhere.

'We might look in now,' said the ICU man. 'They've probably done their bit.'

'Their bit?'

'Defibrillation. Intubation. That sort of thing. If he hasn't come round, I should just slide in an IV line and give him the usual.'

'Okay.'

'So I'll be off.'

'Thanks.'

Campbell went in. The patient, an obese grey-haired man in his sixties, lay on his back. His colour was good. . . . He was not dead. One of the nurses bent over his head, feeling the carotid pulse at the angle of the jaw with one hand, and pumping a ventilation bag with the other. Her colleague stood holding two large chest electrodes connected to a red shock box.

'How is he?'

'Okay.'

'What's his rhythm?'

'Sinus. Now.'

'Coming round?'

'I think so. . . . Bugger him.'

'Why bugger him?'

'Well, I shocked him three times. . . .'

'What's wrong with that?'

'I needed four.'

'Four for what?'

'To make twenty for my defibrillation badge.'

'Never mind,' said Campbell, quoting a remark he had heard at several resuscitation attempts. 'You can't win 'em all.'

The nurse looked at him as though he had made a joke in very poor taste. The patient was coughing and gagging on his endotracheal tube. The nurse at his head whipped it out and said rather matter of factly, 'You're all right now, Mr Marquis, you just fainted.'

'Did I?' said the patient. 'It feels like someone was dancing on my chest while I was out.'

'Here's doctor to have a wee word with you,' said the nurse.

Campbell, taken by surprise, muttered something about a faint caused by the heart missing a beat or two. The nurse at the top of the patient hissed quietly at him, 'We don't mention hearts to coronary patients. Unit policy.'

Campbell reasserted his authority by pulling out his stethoscope and listening to the patient's heart with an expression of the utmost concentration and gravity on his face for fully a minute. When the nurses were beginning to get restive he put his stethoscope away, pursed his lips and said thoughtfully, 'There's just a suggestion of reversed splitting of the second sound.' The nurses glanced uncertainly at each other and the patient broke the silence by saying, 'Thank you, doctor. Thanks very much. I can't thank you enough for what you've done.'

Feeling it would be difficult to improve on that, Campbell acknowledged the patient's thanks, left them to it and went off to the doctor's duty room where, it was to be hoped, he would spend his night on duty undisturbed.

On his way to the intensive care unit Campbell had looked in at the research fellows' room to pick up his notes on the faecal vitamin pilot study and had found on his desk a thick monograph called 'Vitamin Assay: a Manual of Laboratory Techniques' by someone called Snodgrass who had as many letters after his name as the late Emperor of Abyssinia. Attached there was the now customary 'With Compliments' slip bearing Rosamund's name in print and her secretary's scribbled initials below. On finding it Campbell wondered if she had checked up on whether he had put in an appearance at the vitamin assay laboratory where he was supposed to be setting up the method for colonic specimens, and resolved to have coffee with the technician there at the first possible opportunity, which would be on Monday morning. And he had brought Snodgrass's manual down to intensive care because while on duty he could not leave the unit, and he had gathered from others on the rota that a night there was a good chance to get down to some solid reading.

Snodgrass ran to four hundred pages, not counting the forty pages of references at the back. The preface to the fourth edition thanked friends and colleagues the world over for a wealth of comment and suggestion on the previous edition, as did the preface to the third and the second editions. The preface to the first edition stated piously that in an area of laboratory work where practice varied so widely, with differing techniques and clinical requirements, it was presumptuous for one worker, of necessarily limited experience, to attempt a comprehensive survey. Nonetheless. . . .

Campbell sat in the duty room browsing forward into the text. He learned from page two hundred and three that in the bio-assay technique for phytamenadione estimation which used newborn rats, the diet of their mothers during pregnancy was crucial to the accuracy of the method. Not only were standard vitamin supplements mandatory, but any vegetable products of the genus *Brassica* (kale, sprouts, cabbage, cauliflower and many other greens) were to be strictly avoided. The diet of the mothers prior to conception was less important, though some workers had reported related difficulties (Refs 1189-1193). Campbell tried to remember whether Rosamund had said anything in her introductory chat about looking after rat mothers-to-be.

The duty room was, by the standards of doctors' accommodation in the Institute, not unpleasant. It was furnished with a desk, a couple of armchairs and a television set and in a little curtained alcove a fold-up bed was already made up for the night. There was a fresh towel by the wash hand basin and a tired-looking piece of evil-smelling yellow soap. Beside the desk was a filing cabinet with drawers cryptically labelled 'Results 1963-1967', 'Dr Cromwell's Lipid Project 1958' and 'Scottish and Newcastle Study'. Campbell tried the last named drawer. It was unlocked, and half full of cans of beer. Duty in the intensive care unit might not be too bad after all. He skimmed on through Snodgrass, and drank a can or two of beer.

At about seven o'clock there was a knock on the door. Campbell threw his empty cans rather noisily into the waste paper basket and said 'Come in'. An auxiliary did so, carrying his evening meal on a tray. She was wearing pink rubber gloves smelling of disinfectant.

'There you are, doctor,' she said, leaning over him to put it down on the desk in front of him. Campbell rescued Snodgrass, put him to one side and removed the aluminium cover from his plate. Somehow, the cover was searingly hot and the stew, cabbage and potato underneath almost cold. He left them and turned to the tinned fruit and ice-cream, which was melting. The only other edible item on the tray was a sliver of plastic-wrapped cheese. The tea (tea!) provided was cold, so he reached over to the filing cabinet for another can.

After dinner he switched on the television and sat back in one of the armchairs. An emergent African politician consisting of a white smile and the occasional flicker of eyeball was being interviewed in a dark hut by a man in a safari suit. The other programme was advertising sliced bread. He switched the set off and went back to his vitamins.

Just after nine o'clock there was a short high-pitched buzz behind him and disembodied female voice said, 'Dr Campbell, there's a small anterior on its way down from Casualty.' Campbell turned round just in time to see the orange light below the intercom loudspeaker going off.

'Doctor Campbell.' The light came on again. 'You've got to speak while the light's on.'

'All right.'

'Doctor Campbell, there's a small anterior coming down from Casualty.'

'All right.'

'All right.'

Campbell thought about the message and decided it meant that a new admission, a patient whose identity and sex were unknown or unimportant, but of whom it was known that he or she had suffered a slight coronary thrombosis affecting the front of the heart, was about to come in to the unit. He put down his book and went through to the monitoring area.

It was in darkness except for a small reading lamp at the console, and the various pulse indicator lights and the ECG display oscilloscopes, whose brilliant green blips flicked across their screens tracing the rhythm of each frail or suspect heart. One nurse was working in a dimly lit cubicle, and the other was sitting at the desk knitting, glancing from time to time over the array of screens and lights in front of her. Campbell went across and stood a little behind her, looking at the tracings. Without turning round she said, 'We usually just get you when we're ready for you to see the new patients.'

'Oh. Everything okay?'

'Number three had a couple of VEs. Looked like he was brewing an R on T. He's got Mexilitene running in, so we just speeded it up for ten minutes.'

'Seems reasonable.'

The door of the monitoring area opened and a man was wheeled in. He was wired up to a small electrocardiographic monitor sitting on a special shelf at the foot of his trolley. A lady in a fur coat, carrying an artificial leg under her arm, followed, completing the little procession.

'He was going kind of fast on the way down,' said the porter to Campbell.

'That's lovely now just take a seat outside please,' said one of the nurses to the lady in the fur coat.

'Will he be needing his leg in here?'

'No. Not until he gets out and up to the wards. Just take it with you.'

'But . . . he sort of likes it near him even when he's not wearing it.'

'It would get in the way. That's lovely now just take a seat outside please.'

'Will he be needing his false teeth?'

The nurse snatched a pink heart-shaped plastic container from the lady's hand and ushered her out. The man was wheeled into an empty cubicle and lifted bodily on to the bed. Before the portable monitor was disconnected he was stripped to his underpants and one of the nurses, producing from nowhere a large pair of electric clippers, began to shave his chest, leaving neat little circles of hair round each nipple. He was wired up by limb and chest leads to the ICU monitoring system, and the smaller one was disconnected. Since his arrival in the unit no one had yet addressed the patient directly.

The porter took the trolley and its monitor away, remarking to Campbell as he passed, 'It looked like one of those ventricular tachycardias to me.' Campbell was left alone at the desk watching six sets of displays and readings, hoping fervently that nothing untoward would happen.

After five or ten minutes the nurses came out again. One said to the other, 'These ankle straps just weren't designed for mid-thigh stumps,' and then to Campbell, 'This is when we normally call you.' He took that as his cue and went in to see his new admission, who turned out to be a butcher from a village a little way out into the country. He was not at all awed by his situation ('Of course we see all this on the television now.') and talked calmly about his previous medical history ('I left one leg near Cherbourg, as you can see.'). He seemed more concerned as to the whereabouts of his artificial limb than he was about his episode of chest pain which, he insisted, his own doctor had cured at home with an injection.

Campbell was agreeably surprised to find himself once more enjoying clinical medicine. He did the history and examination and wrote up the case, then discussed with the nurses the finer points of the patient's electrocardiogram without demonstrating too much in the way of ignorance. They offered him a cup of coffee and, feeling he had now justified his presence on the unit, he accepted it. The three talked for a while then the night duty nurses arrived and it was made clear to Campbell that he should go back to his room.

Tired by the various excesses of the day, and anticipating a night broken by calls to the ICU patients, Campbell went to bed early and started to read himself to sleep with Snodgrass on thiamine estimation. It was just beginning to work when his bedside telephone rang.

'Dr Campbell.'

'David. . . . Jean here.'

'Oh. How did you know I was here?'

'You mentioned it. On the grass a few days ago.'

'Did I?'

'Yes. . . . David, there are a couple of results you might be interested in. Came in this afternoon . . . while you were off sick.'

He could sense her amusement on the other end of the phone. 'Oh?'

'Yes. Mrs Herron. Her prothrombin time's come down. It's rather good now.'

When Campbell had been a resident it had not been his practice to ring up his superiors at quarter past ten in the evening just to tell them some routine lab results.

'And there's another one. A blood result. I don't know the patient but the writing on the form is definitely you.'

'What's the patient's name?'

'Alexander.'

'Christian name?'

'It doesn't say.'

'Male or female?'

'You haven't filled in that bit of the form either.'

'Oh. Anything interesting?'

'Haemoglobin low normal. ESR a bit high. Forty. Funny differential though.'

'What does it show?'

'An awful lot of eosinophils.'

'Really?'

'What's the patient got?'

'What?'

'What's the diagnosis?'

There was a silence in which Campbell tried to work out which patient he was supposed to be thinking about, as a first step towards diagnosis. 'Oh. One of Ratho's clinic. Ulcerative colitis.'

'Do you get eosinophils in that?'

'Mmmm. I'm not sure. I don't think so.'

'What do you get them in?' Jean asked.

'Allergic things. Hay fever.'

'Has she got that too?'

'She didn't mention it.' Perhaps she would have mentioned it to Dr Ratho, because he was so understanding.

'You get eosinophils in other things too, don't you?'

Campbell's little stock of eosinophil-related knowledge was fast running out. 'Tropical eosinophilia?' he suggested with a sense of despair.

'D'you get that in Edinburgh?' said Jean, rather crushingly.

'Hang on. She travels a lot. On ships.'

'What's tropical eosinophilia?'

'I don't know,' said Campbell. 'Except that you get lots of eosinophils in it.' He could hear her laughing.

'What about parasites?' said Jean. 'They give you eosinophils.'

'Parasites in one of Fraser Ratho's awfully nice lady patients? They wouldn't dare.'

'Maybe they would. Especially if she's been abroad. What's she like clinically?'

'Fit-looking in a seedy, tanned way. About forty. Not getting enough.'

'How d'you know that?'

'She jumped around like a gogo dancer to show me her tan. And then told me she'd had her uterus out.'

'Poor David. Did your stethoscope twitch?'

'Not much. I closed my eyes and thought of the General Medical Council.' He could hear her laughing again.

'What else has she got?'

'Feels generally grotty. With the usual colitis symptoms. Some blood. Not much slime. Doing moderately but not spectacularly well on salazopyrine.'

There was a pause then they both said, at exactly the same time and practically shouting, 'Amoebiasis!'

'And she doesn't have ulcerative colitis at all!' said Jean.

'Bingo!'

'It was *Entamoeba Histolytica* all the time!'

'That's the fellow.'

'How are you going to prove it?' Jean asked. 'What does the barium look like? Has she been sigmoidoscoped? There should be a biopsy report somewhere. . . .'

Campbell felt like a resident being battered backwards on to the ropes by an exceptionally keen registrar. He said, 'Steady on,' deciding he would get Jean to find the notes and bring them down, so that they could check on what diagnostic tests had been and what others would have to be done to prove their theory. He would therefore get up and pretend he hadn't been to bed. 'Jean, if you go into the secretary's office and find the pile of notes for that clinic. She's called Sandra Alexander. Bring them down here and I'll have a look through them. . . .' There was dissenting silence from the other end. 'Where are you? On the ward?'

'No actually. I'm in the Residency. I'm in bed.' Campbell gulped, and found himself wriggling involuntarily between the sheets. 'I thought I'd have an early night. In case they call me a lot.'

'Oh, well. I suppose it can wait till morning.'

'Nights on have been busy all this week. And a couple of people were looking a bit shaky when I went round an hour ago.'

'You poor tired houseman.'

She snorted. 'Anyway, I don't want to get dressed and put on my Scholls and trudge round looking for notes for a power crazed research person. I'm in bed and I'm warm and comfortable.'

Campbell's grip on the phone tightened.

'How's ICU?' she asked.

'All right. Six patients. One new admission. A nice one-legged coronary. A butcher. The nurses wouldn't let him keep his wooden leg under the bed.'

'Poor man. . . . I suppose they are a bit strict.'

'How do you know?'

'I used to work there. As a nursing auxiliary when I was a wee girl in fourth year medicine. I did it every vac.'

'Like it?'

'It was nice. The staff nurses taught me how to read ECGs. Just to annoy the doctors.'

'What did you do apart from reading ECGs?'

'Auxiliary things. I liked it. I used to have to make the doctor's breakfast and take it into the duty room.'

'Did you?'

'I always made scrambled eggs. But it didn't matter 'cos it was a different doctor every day. I used to get embarrassed taking it in. Sometimes I had to wake the chap up, and sometimes he'd be lying in bed, looking at me and my scrambled eggs.'

Campbell recalled the manner in which his dinner had arrived. Compare and contrast. 'Anyone we know?'

'Oh, yes. Lots of people. It's funny coming back here as a houseman. I still get strange "Didn't you used to make my breakfast" looks. Fraser Ratho's one. He used to wear the sweetest tartan print pyjamas.'

Campbell, who was not wearing anything, wondered what she was wearing. Nothing for speed, most likely, like most housemen. Up, dressed and across to the ward in no time, a dozen suffering times a night if your luck was out. 'I'll think of you when my breakfast comes.'

'Goodnight, David. See you in the morning.'

'Goodnight.'

Campbell put the phone down, switched off the light and lay back in the dark, with Jean's voice still gentle and sweet in his ears. He thought of her lying in the Residency, very likely in the bed that he himself had occupied the year before, as rooms were allocated by ward appointments. What was she thinking?

There was a great deal about the phone call that Campbell did not understand. She had phoned him up, late at night and after she had gone to bed, about two minor pieces of information neither of which needed immediate action and both of which could have waited perfectly well until the next morning. Not that he minded of course. The easy rapport of the phone call, and its sleepy free-floating, midnight-intimate ending were an advance even on their time together the first day on the lawn. They had both been in bed, probably both naked, and though separated by a few hundred yards of telephone wire and half a dozen grim institutional walls, had once again strayed together into each other's thoughts.

Campbell turned on his side, imagining her naked nearness, and as he did so Snodgrass slid from his bed and thumped leadenly to the floor.

He slept badly. Jean, naked and sometimes carrying a plate of scrambled eggs, alternated in his dreams with such cataclysmic images as a nuclear holocaust precipitated by a mad staff nurse pressing the wrong button. In his dreams he was called to resuscitate furiously alive patients and decaying corpses, including one called Jim. At three in the morning a very real staff nurse came and woke him to tell him that the butcher had had another massive anterior and was dead. Campbell got up and certified the body then went back to bed. The rest of his night's dreaming was liberally spattered with artificial limbs.

A middle-aged auxiliary, malodorous and faintly moustached, brought his breakfast in at eight o'clock. He lay and looked at her and thought of Jean, then got up and dressed and did a quick round in ICU. Apart from being one day older, the patients were all exactly as he had found them. The two staff nurses who had been on a late duty together had returned on an early, completing the illusion of changelessness. Campbell went back to the duty room to find the bed packed away, the chairs rearranged and his passable tally of empty beer cans gone from the waste paper basket. Had anyone counted them?

The doctor who had recruited Campbell in the first place, and handed over to him the night before, reappeared at two minutes past nine, remarking that he was glad to see that Campbell had had a quiet night. To put the record straight, he was told about the butcher, the wooden leg and the lady in the fur coat.

'I expect she'll be up some time in the course of the morning,' he said as Campbell gathered up his toothbrush and razor.

Campbell reached the medical library at ten past nine, with the intention of doing a little solid reading before going to the ward. The man who edited the textbook was sitting scribbling away from a mound of reference books, looking as if he had been there for hours, or possibly even worked right through from closing time on Friday night. The mouse prostaglandin lady came in only a few minutes after Campbell, followed by Jocasta Smith, who gave him a large stagey smile. Was she showing approval of his masochistically early Saturday morning start, or had she simply had a good run of breasts, or was she still thanking him for the piece that he had not in any case given her? Being seen there by her Campbell felt a little fraudulent, never having been in the library on a Saturday morning before, at any hour.

When he went up to the ward Jean was in her room. She seemed glad to see him.

'Busy last night?' he enquired.

'Not called at all. It was lovely. The first night that's happened since I started here. How was ICU?'

'The butcher died.'

'The one-legged one?'

'Yes. It was sad.'

'In the middle of the night?'

'About three.'

'Anyone else come in?'

'No. But I didn't sleep well. And breakfast was horrible.'

'It wouldn't have been if I'd made it for you.'

They both smiled. Despite having been seeing her on and off for several days and either thinking about her or dreaming of her more or less continuously for the previous twelve hours, Campbell found that there were still breathtaking discoveries to be made in her eyes and face and voice. As he looked at her her left eyebrow came down a tiny bit and he knew she was going to talk about a patient, most likely the lady with suspected amoebiasis. 'Now about . . .' he began.

'Mrs Alexander. . . . I've got her notes.'

'Good.'

She reached round to her desk to pick them up. 'I had a quick look through them. She's been . . . fairly lightly investigated.'

'Meaning not very thoroughly investigated.'

'I'm afraid so. Even when she was in the ward.'

'Is there a biopsy?'

'Not really,' said Jean.

'Either there is or there isn't,' said Campbell, sounding, he knew, a bit like Bones doing his decisive-surgeon make-up-your-mind thing.

'There isn't. There's a note saying "For sigmoidoscopy and biopsy", then another one saying "Sigmoidoscopy: Characteristic ulcerations at ten centimetres".'

'Does one ask who?'

'Dr Ratho,' said Jean.

'Is he around this morning?' asked Campbell, who was quite looking forward to exploring with his superior, the aforementioned dilatory physician, the various diagnostic possibilities left by his sketchy handling of the case.

'I haven't seen him.'

'Anyway we need a biopsy.'

'Because the radiological appearances are non-specific,' said Jean.

'And an examination of a specimen of stool.'

'Fresh stool,' Jean added.

'And I suppose she ought to have liver function tests,' said Campbell.

'Because they get liver abscesses . . .'

'Commonly in the right lobe . . .'

'Posteriorly. . . .'

'Which may rupture. . . .'

'Into the chest. . . .'

'Giving rise to dramaticce symptoms. . . .'

'Including fever. . . .'

'And cough. . . .'

'With the production of characteristic anchovy-paste sputum,' they chanted in unison, both laughing.

'You've been reading it up.'

'Just a glance.'

'Me too.'

'Anyway,' said Campbell, 'now we're all experts, I'll mention it to Ratho. He'll probably have to bring her in again. That'll be nice. Rub his nose in it a bit.'

She screwed up her face. 'Don't gloat. We all make mistakes. And anyway it still might not be.'

'We don't all deserve mistakes the way he does,' said Campbell. 'Serves him right for making me do his clinic.'

'Come on, David. You'd rather look at patients than do research.'

Campbell thought about that, then said, 'I don't know. I haven't done any.'

Jean started making purposeful gestures with a tray of blood-letting things and Campbell felt suddenly superfluous. It was almost time for the early Saturday morning coffee which was traditional upstairs on Creech's unit while the grand old gentleman orbited with obsessional sloth round the ward below. Bertram was there in Sister's room with Roddy Abavana, who was talking animatedly, and flashing eloquent pink palms. 'Of course my decision to stay in Western Deep Levels and even for that matter Tweefonteins was not reached easily. It is no small matter, particularly for an African, to have holdings in such affairs. But I asked myself who would suffer first, longest and most severely from any recession there. Would it not be the toilers, the black people, the people like me? Particularly after Sharpeville, when confidence in every undertaking was badly shaken and prices fell dramatically. In fact my family at that time picked up two hundred Hartebeests for a matter of shillings rather than pounds. Shortly afterwards confidence returned. I like to think that we did our bit in the only way that we could from the distance. Hello, David.'

'Hello, Roddy.'

'Hello, young Campbell. You look as if you need a coffee.'

'If you will please excuse me,' said Roddy. 'You must not think me rude, but I have a few phone calls to make.' He smiled broadly. 'The market closes but the watchers listen.'

As he went out Bertram looked wonderingly after him and let out a puff of pipe smoke with a moist smacking noise. 'When I was a lad at Sunday school, we used to put money in a wee straw box like a hut with a slot in the roof. You used to take it round rattling it and saying "Pennies for the wee black babies". I often wondered what happened to them.'

Campbell laughed, not simply because Bertram was three years his senior, and his superior by one or two rungs on the hierarchy. 'What's he supposed to be doing here?'

'I don't think he's ever troubled to ask,' said Bertram. 'But he'll be set for professor when he goes back. . . . Anyway, young Campbell, how about yourself? Back at last from sickbed and exile.'

'All right.'

'Vitamins, isn't it?'

'That's it.'

'With Rosamund?'

'Right.'

'How's it going?'

'Taking it gently to begin with. Old Creech said that was the correct approach.'

'Creech. . . . As opposed to Rosamund.'

'Rosamund hasn't said much since I started.'

'Well, knowing her, she might begin to.'

'I suppose so. . . . I do have one or two things in the offing. The colonic mucosa stuff is poised for its first specimen. And the reading's . . . coming along.'

'Ah well. . . . And how's the clinical side?'

'That's fun,' said Campbell, hoping the change of tone wasn't too obvious. He was about to tell Bertram about the impending diagnostic coup in the case of Sandra Alexander when he remembered the circumstances in which he had acquired her. 'There's some interesting stuff about. . . . Is Dr Ratho around this morning?'

Bertram emitted triplet smoke-puffs then dispersed them with the rest of the inhalation. 'No, he's not. There was something he mentioned. Ah yes. He's taking a week off. And he'd like you to see to Dr Creech's colitis clinics for him on Tuesday and Thursday. Just this coming week.'

'Really?'

'He said you'd know the ropes.'

'Did he? Where's he off to?'

'Funny you should ask. He's taking a week's leave to paint his house.' Bertram smiled enigmatically through a veil of blue smoke. 'And there's another thing. Dr Creech wanted to ask you himself, but there's no harm in you having a little advance warning. How would you like to increase your clinical commitment in the female ward . . .?' Campbell translated that immediately into time spent with Jean. 'Temporarily?'

'Interesting thought.'

'He mentioned it and said he'd mention it to Rosamund. Meantime I'm mentioning it to you. But wait till he mentions it.'

'And don't mention that you've mentioned it? You mean look after Creech's female beds instead of Ratho while he's off?' Campbell brightened. 'Great. Thanks a lot.'

'Don't mention it,' said Bertram. 'It might be a useful little spell. Especially if you're keen and make a good job of it.'

'Really?'

'Well, frankly. . . . Fraser's all right and a nice chap. . . .'

'But . . .?'

'Exactly. You're not very experienced, but if you're keen and careful, and ask about things you're not sure of . . . you could hardly go wrong.'

'Really?'

'Fraser's mind hasn't entirely been on his work.'

'No?' Campbell remembered the paint on his hands.

'And then there are his . . . family problems.'

'Really?'

'Have you met his wife?'

'No.'

'He only married her because she asked him nicely and he thought it wouldn't be very nice to say no and anyway she's bigger than he is.'

Campbell listened happily to Bertram's views on this and many other topics and had several cups of coffee while waiting for Creech and his unexpected invitation to increase his clinical commitment. When Creech arrived and it came, he accepted it, having been reassured by Creech that it had been discussed with Rosamund who had agreed that the additional experience would be useful to Campbell, and yet not so prolonged or burdensome as to affect in any significant way his primary commitment to research.

Later that morning Campbell went along to the unit secretary's office to sign his letters from Ratho's Thursday clinic. The secretary handed them over, remarking, 'Everyone starts off by being prompt with their letters. Especially those with small clinics.' He signed them, lingering proudly over their stiff, official phrases (She might derive considerable benefit from a modest increase in her dosage of salazopyrine. May I suggest . . .). When he gave them back to her for posting she said, 'I hear you'll be doing the clinic next week too.'

'Yes. Dr Ratho's taking most of the week off.'

'And you're looking after Dr Creech's female beds as well?'

'Yes.' How did she know that?

'You're a bit junior.'

'Dr Bertram said he'd help me with anything I wasn't sure about.'

'Did he?'

'Yes.'

'Aren't you supposed to be almost full time research?'

'Yes. But if Fraser Ratho's off, someone's got to look after the beds. Dr Bertram seems to think it'll be okay.'

'He would.'

'Would he? I mean, why shouldn't it be okay?'

'Did he say anything about Dr Ratho's study leave?'

'Study leave?'

'It went through as study leave. That's what was on the

application form that Dr Creech signed.'

'What's he studying for?'

'He just mentioned doing some general reading. And preparing himself for an interview.'

'I thought he was painting his house.' Campbell wasn't sure what he was trying to find out from the secretary, or, for that matter, what she was trying to find out from him. The matter of the interview was a new development. 'What interview?'

'Didn't you know? An honorary lectureship. In place of Dr Elder. The interview's a week on Monday.'

'Really? Who else is in for it?'

'A black man from the Southern.'

'Anyone else?'

'Dr Bertram.'

THREE

Campbell climbed the stairs towards the unit on the Monday of the first full week of his job with a sense of duty left undone. It was half past ten, and he was forced to admit to himself that he ought to have been there at nine and thinking more positively about the colonic mucosa experiment. By half past ten he should have captured a specimen from one of the operating theatres and been hard at work in the vitamin assay lab. But that in turn would have necessitated a Sunday evening trip down the surgical corridor, checking on the lists for the following day, in search of likely sources of material. Though this had occurred to Campbell on Sunday afternoon, he had not exerted himself and somehow another day's progress seemed to have slipped from his grasp already.

An odd little group was coming down the stair towards him. There were three young men and a woman. One of the men was carrying a polythene bag containing toilet things and clothes – nightdresses, a dressing gown and the like – of various pastel colours. The woman, who was middle-aged, was being supported by the other two men. She was weeping, and the men were also clearly upset. As they passed Campbell recognised them. They were the coalmen grandsons of Mrs Innes, not dressed for work, but clean and spruce in collars, ties and sports jackets. Their ties were black. The one carrying the bundle of clothes appeared to be crying.

'Morag Hamilton was called out to certify her at six this morning. I was off for the weekend. Apparently she had another stroke, a big one down the other side. Happened on Saturday afternoon and extended on Sunday. . . . Poor old dear. The family was really fond of her.'

For the first time, Campbell saw Jean looking hard pressed. She was scribbling laboratory request forms in automatic haste, while answering a question about something else and possibly worrying about something else again. A lot of the feeling of being a houseman came back. Not highly recommended, even as a spectator sport.

'Are you pushed?'

'A bit. Dr Kyle was due five minutes ago. And I've still got heaps to do.' She was ticking off every investigation offered in an extremely comprehensive clinical chemistry request form. 'I don't know what they want to know her SHBD for. . . . Oh. Dr Bertram came in this morning and told me you're taking over Dr Creech's female beds.'

'Only for a week. For the redecoration of Chateau Ratho.'

'What? Oh. That'll be good.'

'I'm a bit worried.'

'Dr Bertram said you were but you needn't be.'

'That was nice of him.'

'We've to let him know if we need help.'

'He said that.'

'And there's always Dr Creech.'

'So there is. It's funny how you forget that.'

Jean was scribbling an X-ray request form. Even when she wrote very quickly her writing was clear and, in a simple, functional way, beautiful.

'And when would you like to go round your beds, sir?'

'Watch it. When would suit you?'

'Two?'

'I've got an out-patient.'

'Three?'

'That would be nice. How many patients has Creech got?'

'Eight and some empty beds.'

'Plus Rosamund's three. . . .'

'Two and an empty bed.'

'Eight plus two and some empty beds. Power at last. See you at three.'

'See you at three.'

Campbell went for coffee and thence to the research fellows' room, where he sat and read his *Guardian*, while Dilys knitted her way through another isotope test seventeen rows at a time, and Roddy scanned the financial pages and made several of his cryptic specialist phone calls. The gospel of vitamin assay according to Snodgrass lay closed and reproachful on Campbell's desk. Rather than open it he dug out the notes from his original conversation with Rosamund, together with the list of references she had sent, and started to regroup the various headings, expanding some with notes and thoughts of his own, in his most serious effort so far at organising himself for an assault into the unknown. The longer he worked at it the less exciting was the prospect of his proposed year ('In the first instance only of course . . . If, as seems likely, you get interested and show talent for this sort of thing, there should be no trouble in getting you some more funds to continue and another technician and perhaps support for another research fellow. A Faecal Vitamin Unit is a real possibility for the year after next. . . .').

After half an hour there was a strong and growing suspicion that part of the unknown allotted to him for assault was unknown because it was unlikely to prove either interesting or important. Did Rosamund know this? Was she sending him off to explore a small cul-de-sac, far from the frontiers of clinical science, just for the sake of completeness? Or was she genuinely convinced that there were possibilities in the area : possibilities, that is, of results and hence publications, by Fyvie and somebody and somebody else and Campbell, leading to greater fame for her, and the nearer prospect of the professorial chair she coveted so much? An opportunist assessment covering both these possibilities would have been fairly typical of Rosamund's approach. Campbell thought about it, and decided that the most likely thing was that the drug company which supported him had wanted to off-load some money, for tax purposes or for the general hoorah-effect of supporting medical research, and Rosamund had heard about it and thrown the project together on a sheet of foolscap one evening at home, between feeding the beagles and rubbing down the horses, on the basis of ideas which, it was rumoured, had originated with Dr Elder, late honorary lecturer, now general practitioner. He finished a complex doodle of Heath

Robinson scientific apparatus, and got up to stretch his legs.

There was time before lunch for a stroll through the hospital and a browse along the surgical corridor to see what was brewing in the way of colonic surgery for Tuesday's lists. Campbell swithered between that and a token visit to the vitamin assay lab, and eventually decided that he could fit in both if he didn't loiter, and didn't mind delaying lunch until about quarter past twelve, at which time a chance encounter in the vicinity of the female ward might just lead to lunch with Jean.

'Hello.'

'Hello.'

'Good weekend?'

'Okay.'

'Parents all right?'

'Fine. How was ICU on Friday?'

'The staff nurses bullied me.'

'Who?'

'They didn't introduce themselves. A wee thin one and big one with psoriasis on one elbow.'

'Oh. Joyce and Cathy. They're nice.'

'They weren't nice to me.'

'You probably frightened them. I'm going down there on a late now. I'll get all the "That dreadful Dr Campbell you used to go out with" stuff.'

'Tough.'

'I'm probably more used to it than you think.'

'Oh.' There was a silence and, mainly because he couldn't think of anything else to say, Campbell said, 'Friday was nice.'

'You did all right. For a sick man,' said Joan quietly. Campbell, always a sucker for sexual flattery, suggested she might like to come round to the flat for a coffee or something when she came off her late duty. She said she would.

Mrs Alexander may have been on time for her appointment but Campbell was three minutes late, having been detained over coffee on the lawn by Jocasta Smith. His patient was sitting in the corridor outside the out-patient consulting room.

Even in passing her to go into the room Campbell noted a change in her appearance: she was more sallow and also, it seemed, more haggard and wrinkled than she had been the previous week.

There was no nurse, though one had been arranged, and no battery for the viewing light attached to the sigmoidoscope. It was ten past two when he asked Mrs Alexander to come in. Before she raised the topic of Dr Ratho, he did.

'I'm afraid I must present Dr Ratho's apologies again, Mrs Alexander. He's taken study leave.' Campbell decided that it would have been unprofessional to explain exactly what he had taken study leave for.

'He's a wonderful young man. Brilliant, I hear.'

Not from me, thought Campbell. 'He is exceptionally dedicated.'

'Anyway,' she said with a smile, another instant high-voltage job, 'I have every confidence in you too, Dr Cameron.'

'Dr Campbell.'

'Dr Campbell. Sorry. And to tell you the truth I'm feeling so ill I almost don't mind who I see.'

'I noticed you were looking less well.'

'I feel terrible. I've had a lot of pain. As well as the usual things. And I'm going much oftener.'

'The bowels?'

'All the time, Dr Campbell.'

'Blood.'

'Quite a lot.'

'Slime.'

'Sometimes.'

'How's your appetite?'

'Not a thing, Dr Campbell. Usually I have to watch everything. But not now. The pounds are simply pouring off me.'

'D'you feel bad all the time?'

'Yes. And worse sometimes. Hot. I feel much worse than I've ever felt since I first started with my colitis. Even worse than before I came in the last time.'

She looked awful: red-eyed and dry-mouthed, like someone with a monster hangover. Sallow folds hung round her neck, wrinkled like cracked mud.

'May I examine your abdomen, Mrs Alexander?' This time

she was less spry getting up on the couch. Her belly was hot to the touch. She was diffusely tender over the large bowel, and when he put the edge of his hand along the border of the ribs on the right and asked her to breathe in she flinched quite a bit. Her liver was enlarged and tender. Campbell palpated it gently first with one hand then with two, using his left to try and bring it forward in her abdomen to find out if there was anything going on posteriorly in the right lobe. Then he felt for her spleen. It too was enlarged and tender. He sat at the desk and noted down the new developments in the case-folder. As he did so the nurse took her temperature.

'Thirty-eight five. Pulse a hundred and eight.'

'How would you feel about coming in again, Mrs Alexander?'

'Really, Dr Campbell, I'd be glad to.'

'Could you come in this afternoon?'

'I'd like to go home and get my things.'

'How long would that take?'

'An hour or so.'

'Is there someone with you?'

'Yes. My sister-in-law.'

'It'll be ward three again. Just like before. Dr Creech will be your consultant again.'

'Who?'

'Dr Creech. The senior consultant.'

'Oh. . . . When's Dr Ratho coming back?'

'Perhaps the end of the week.'

'Oh . . .? No. . . . I'll come in today. . . . Does that mean you won't be doing that sigmo thing?'

'Not until you come in.'

She grimaced again, most unattractively. Campbell reflected that the geometry of sigmoidoscopy more or less precluded looking at the patient's face while one was doing it.

'Jean?'

'Hello, David.'

'I'm bringing in a patient from out-patients.'

'Yes, Dr Campbell.' She was sitting at her desk. Her face tilted slightly to one side, with a wry smile. 'And what please is the patient's name?'

'Oh, the amoeba lady. Mrs Alexander.'

'D'you still think she's got it?'

'Could well be.'

'Is she ill?'

'Fairly. Hot. Dry. Big sore liver. And a spleen.'

'D'you think she's got an abscess?'

'Maybe.'

'Has she got a cough with the production of characteristic anchovy paste sputum?'

'D'you know, I forgot to ask. But I'm sure she'd have mentioned it.' They were both smiling at their new private joke.

'Are these her notes?' She took them and opened them at Campbell's latest entry, which consisted of the date, half a dozen scrawled words and a wild sketch of an abdomen with liver, spleen and colon roughly cross-hatched to denote tenderness. Jean read out, 'Ill. Scrawny. Dry. Hot. Query amoeba. Query query abscess. T.C.I. What's T.C.I.?'

'To come in.'

'Oh. . . . It'll be nice being post-registration next year.'

'Why?'

'Keeping awful notes. And feeling superior about it.'

'Watch it.'

'Yes, Dr Campbell.'

'Have you been for tea?'

'No, Dr Campbell.' She stood up. 'Come on, David. Let's go round Rosamund's lot first, then go for tea.'

From unconsidered habit they went first to the spot a little beyond the nursing station where Mrs Innes had lived and died. Bed and locker were formidably and inhumanly neat and tidy. A temperature chart with a large pink star and 'Dr Rosamund Fyvie' printed on it, but no patient's name and no readings marked up, hung from a hook on the wall behind, awaiting the next incumbent. They paused silently as colonial visitors might beside the Cenotaph in Whitehall, then Jean said, 'Have you got anyone T.C.I.?'

'I'll look at the W.L. It's sad. I liked her.'

'So did the nurses. She used to give them humbugs.'

The only development Campbell knew of in the case of Mrs Herron, the jaundiced lady with primary biliary cirrhosis, was

the improvement in her blood clotting mechanisms as reflected in her more normal prothrombin time. As they got near
her bed, he mused aloud to Jean, 'Are we thinking about
repeating the liver biopsy here?'

'We were. But Dr Fyvie saw her and thought that since
three were inconclusive it was unlikely that another would
add much.'

'Oh. I thought that was what we were aiming for. When
did she see her?'

'Friday. Morning.'

'Oh. So what had she in mind?'

'She said something about a more definitive diagnostic pro-
cedure. She said she'd let you know the details later.'

'Well, she knows where to find me.'

'And Mrs Herron still feels awful. Itching a lot. We've
started her on cholestyramine.'

Campbell resolved to go and look that up too. The patient
was smiling. 'The new stuff's helped a lot. My skin's ever so
much better. The stuff tastes like sand and sawdust, but it's
working wonders. Does that mean I'm getting better?'

'If you feel better, you're improving,' said Campbell. Mrs
Herron's smile faded a little.

'My husband's very pleased too. And my tummy's gone
down a bit.'

'Good.'

'So what's going to happen?'

'Well. . . . Dr Fyvie wants just another test done.'

'Another biopsy in my liver?'

'No. Not exactly.'

'Oh. What then? And when?'

'The details are a little . . . technical. But it'll probably be
later in the week.'

'Will it hurt?'

'I shouldn't think so.'

'Thanks, Dr Campbell.'

Theresa, the girl from St Cuthbert's Hospital, was sitting up
in bed knitting something that looked as if it might turn out
to be a patch for a red string vest. She stopped when the

doctors approached, and beamed a moist myopic smile at Jean.

'Everything all right?' Campbell enquired of Jean.

'I think so.'

'How's Bill's ploy coming along?'

'The KM drug one?'

'No. The isotope thing he wanted to repeat.'

'Oh that. I don't think the fresh stuff has arrived yet.'

'She's all right then?'

'More or less.'

'D'you think her hair's getting thinner?'

'I hadn't noticed.'

'Of course thin brittle hair is part of the syndrome.'

'Along with myopia and simian palmar creases,' said Jean.

'With brachycephaly and a prominent epicanthic fold.'

'What a clever doctor.'

'Okay. But I think it's thinner than before.'

'D'you think so.'

Jean leaned towards the girl, who smiled and laughed. She lifted a strand of the patient's shortish, mouse-brown hair. It came away in her hand. 'Oh. That's new. I wonder what's going on.'

'They do have a high incidence of alopecia areata,' said Campbell, rather grandly.

'Do they?'

'But it might be something to do with the research stuff. The isotope.'

'Bill said the radiation dose was less than you get from a chest X-ray.'

'I wonder. Well, let's wait and see what happens. But I'll mention it to Bill just in case.'

'What about Dr Creech's patients?'

'He's got eight and two empty beds. One when your amoebic abscess lady comes in. But not much happens to most of them. There are five old ladies at the far end, just waiting for this and that. Old people's home places. Beds in long stay wards. That sort of thing.'

'Anyone ill?'

'Not really. An ulcer getting better. Going out soon.'

'Is she on the magic KM ulcer cure?'

'No. Dr Creech isn't keen on it for his patients.'

'Why?'

'Maybe because it's still under evaluation. Or maybe because Rosamund's evaluating it.'

'I see. Anything else?'

'A nice woman with a gall bladder. Settling down on ampicillin.'

'So they're all all right.'

'Yes. Except your lady who isn't in yet.'

'Well, we can whiz round them after tea.'

'All right. Or better still you can whiz round them with the staff nurse while I do a proper admission on Mrs Alexander.'

Dr Creech was having tea alone in Sister's room when they went in for theirs. He was looking just a little bit shifty, and Campbell wondered if he had been having a furtive biscuit-dipping-in-tea session and thought he was about to be caught at it by Sister.

'Good afternoon, sir.'

'Hello, Dr Moray. Hello, Dr Campbell. . . . How are you getting on with the ward work . . .?'

'No great problems so far, sir.'

'It's quiet just now, isn't it? Mainly blocked beds. The acute patients are all right though, aren't they?'

'Yessir.'

'Have I still got two empty beds?'

'I wanted to mention something about that, sir. I saw a patient of yours at Dr Ratho's clinic this afternoon. She was quite ill. In fact I thought she ought to come in.'

'Who was that?'

'A Mrs Alexander.'

'Thin woman? Dyes her hair.'

'Yessir.'

'A bit of a pain in the neck?'

'Slightly, sir, now you mention it.'

'What's wrong with her now?'

'Usual thing, sir. But a little oftener. And some pain recently. She was quite hot and ill. And tender.'

'An exacerbation of her ulcerative colitis?'

'Perhaps, sir.'

'Well, just bring her in and give her the usual.'

'There are one or two odd things about it.' Jean was quietly pouring tea as though to indicate that such matters of high policy were properly outwith her concern.

'What?'

'She's got twenty-five per cent eosinophils.'

'Really . . .? Has she ever been abroad?'

'Quite often, sir. Her husband's at sea.'

'Hmm. Is she having much pain?'

'Yessir. Diffuse. Colicky. Mainly lower abdominal.'

'Mmm. Liver?'

'A bit up. And tender.'

'Might be.'

'What, sir?'

'Amoebiasis.'

Jean handed Campbell a cup of tea, and said to Creech, 'Dr Campbell suggested that as a diagnosis.'

'Hmm. Might be. Especially with the eosinophils. . . . What's the biopsy like?'

Campbell paused. 'We're trying to track one down, sir.'

'Oh. And has anyone looked at a specimen of stool?'

'I don't think so, sir.'

'When's she coming in?'

'This afternoon. Quite soon.'

'Well, if you could have a fresh specimen of stool sent along to my lab as soon as one becomes available. . . .'

'Certainly, sir. But wouldn't it be less trouble just to send it through the routine bacteriology service?'

'It's got to be a fresh specimen. And I'm not sure that any of Professor Swann's staff have ever seen an amoeba. Dead or alive.'

'I suppose it's an uncommon disease. . . .'

'It wasn't in Burma. I used to look at about two hundred slides before breakfast some mornings. That was when the light was best. And I've had the disease myself you know . . .'

Campbell and Jean listened sympathetically throughout a harrowing course of emetine injections. '. . . and there was even one comedian on my hospital staff who used to salute me before he gave the injection, and take one pace back and salute whichever buttock it happened to be that day when he had finished.'

Even before the terminal drollery Jean had been smiling to herself. Campbell wondered if she was thinking, as he had been, about their revered senior physician coughing up gallons and gallons of characteristic anchovy paste sputum.

A stroll with the staff nurse round Dr Creech's patients proved as soothing as even the idlest physician could have wished: there was little to look at, less to say and nothing at all to do. The staff nurse was a pleasant and intelligent girl whom Campbell remembered as a first year nurse with a blue collar. He noted in himself that early symptom of the passing of time, absorbing it into a broader view of the Institute down the years. How many successive blossomings of staff nurses had passed under the old, sad eyes of Henry Creech?

'That lot are no trouble,' said the staff nurse. 'But there are one or two things about Dr Fyvie's.'

'Oh?'

'Yes. Theresa's hair's falling out at a terrible rate. Combfuls yesterday and today.'

'Anything else about her?'

'Not really. Just not so well. A bit peaky.'

'And?'

'Mrs Herron's relations.'

'What about them?'

'They're not exactly up in arms, but they do seem a bit upset. Always asking questions. What's she on? What do the tests show? When's she getting out? That sort of thing.'

'I see. Well, one of us will try and have a word. When do they come up?'

'There's somebody here every visiting hour.'

'Thanks, staff.'

Creech was waiting in the duty room when Campbell returned from his round with the notes. He was wearing a white lab coat, something Campbell had never seen before in two or more years around the unit as student and houseman.

'I thought we'd better settle this question of amoeba in Mrs Alexander. She's a bit awkward and we don't want to be seen to be delaying unnecessarily.'

'No, sir.'

'So I've got a Thermos flask here for the specimen. It has to be kept at blood heat or they just die off, you know. What stage is the patient at?'

'Dr Moray's seeing her now.'

'She's very good, that girl. Of course I knew her father.'

'She seems very conscientious. And the patients like her.'

The doctor in question came in with a tray of instruments and Mrs Alexander's case notes. She glanced with some surprise at Creech's white coat and he explained again about the necessity of settling the amoeba question '. . . so the sooner we get a specimen the better.'

'She's just gone to the loo now,' said Jean.

Creech clutched his Thermos flask. 'You know it's got to be kept at body temperature?'

'Yes, sir. I told the nurse to keep the specimen bottle in warm water just as Dr Campbell said.'

When the sample arrived the three doctors went along to Dr Creech's laboratory. A microscope was set up ready, and half a dozen clean glass slides were ranged on a piece of paper towel along the edge of the bench.

'In case you ever find yourselves doing this,' said Creech, 'it's as well to learn how to do it properly. It's amazing the number of medical graduates who know nothing about it. And yet it's a world-wide problem. Here we are. It's really the mucus that's best. . . . This thing under the microscope is a thing I thought of in Burma and got one of the RAMC technical sergeants to make for me. It maintains everything at about body temperature under the microscope. . . . There we are.'

He was working with an orange stick, deftly manipulating stringy, rather foul mucus on to a slide. Campbell had rarely seen him so absorbed in anything. 'You don't need the highest power. If they're there, you'll see them perfectly well with this.' He spun the disc of objective lenses and adjusted the light, then lifted his spectacles from the bridge of his nose to his forehead, which imparted to his appearance just a suggestion of the military, perhaps of a frail and academic tank commander, with goggles at ease.

'Ah, yes. . . . Hmmm. . . . Yes. There's one. And another. Oh, yes. And another. Mmmm. Yes. And there's one that's just ingested a red cell. They do that you know. They eat red blood cells. And another.'

Creech was twiddling the little knob at the side of the microscope which tracked the slide back and forward as he searched it for parasites. Jean and Campbell watched him, enjoying his enthusiasm, and smiling at the little self-satisfied 'Hmms' he was making at each new discovery below.

'You won't have seen these things, will you?' He beckoned Campbell to the microscope and stood over him, smelling faintly of libraries and laboratories, as he refocused for himself. 'There's a nice one at eleven o'clock, about halfway out from the centre of the field. It's got a red cell inside.'

Down the microscope, in a fragment of mucus from inside a genteel Edinburgh lady, an amoeba was digesting a red cell in the comparative comfort afforded by a clever little water-bath first thought of more than twenty-five years ago by the young Creech, and subsequently constructed by a forgotten sergeant at a hospital in some disputed jungle. The amoeba, large by microscopic standards, perhaps four times as long as its red cell prey, was shapeless but obviously living, its re-fractile, faintly granular cytoplasm bounded by a delicate mobile membrane. It progressed across the field by pouring itself forward in probing advancing folds, and then tucking itself in behind. The red cell which it had enveloped was less distinct in outline than it had been at first. The condemned amoeba ate a hearty meal.

Campbell shifted the slide a little to put the creature back in the centre of the field, and looked up from the microscope.

'D'you see it?' said Creech.

'Yes. Thank you, sir. Very interesting.'

'Dr Moray?'

'Thanks.' Jean moved between Creech and Campbell and bent over the microscope. She adjusted it with her right hand, and put the other on Campbell's shoulder to support herself: a casual gesture, typical of their easiness together, but not one that Campbell could have made without thinking twice. Jean, with her capacity for unreflective intimacy, had been doing that sort of thing quite a lot lately. Like their growing stock of common experience and references, and their un-discussed routines over ward rounds, tea, lunch and so on, it seemed to Campbell something at once precious and fragile, to be enjoyed rather than thought about, and of immediate rather than predictive value. The trusting hand, with its plain gold ring, placed on the shoulder of his white coat in an easy gesture which Campbell knew he could not reciprocate, seemed to him to sum up their relationship.

Campbell looked out over Jean's head and thought about her, with the clean smell of her hair in his nostrils and the weight of her hand on his shoulder. Creech's laboratory windows overlooked the park, green, drowsy and sunlit in the late-summer afternoon. Slanting light sparkled on the slides and the microscope and even picked out a little pointilliste gaiety from the subdued tweed of the jacket hanging behind the door. Once more the little sounds and movements of Jean's breathing seemed the most important things in the universe. Her hand tightened on his shoulder. Campbell glanced at her profile, half hidden by the way her hair had fallen forward. There was no clue in her face as to what she was thinking, whether of him or of the amoeba.

'That pretty well makes the diagnosis,' said Creech. Jean straightened up and as she turned away from the microscope looked briefly at Campbell as though wondering what he was thinking. Once more he was caught unawares, most likely with an expression of at best inane devotion, or, at worst, simply inanity.

'We should go and have a look at the patient. . . . In fact we should have done that first.' Creech smiled shyly, perhaps conscious of his lapse into bad example. 'I'll just wash my hands.'

Jean and Campbell, walking close together, followed him from his lab back to the ward, where he continued to surprise his juniors by a display of clinical expertise, questioning the patient in some detail, confirming Campbell's findings and fielding Mrs Alexander's social hand-grenades with tact and firmness.

The doctors adjourned to the duty room. 'Interesting case,' said Creech. 'She's been to so many places it's hard to say where she's picked it up. Not that it matters. It doesn't seem to spread in this country. We just have to sort her out.'

'What did you make of her liver, sir?' Campbell asked.

'Average. A bit enlarged. A bit tender.'

'We wondered about an abscess.'

'Everybody wonders about that. It's not nearly as common as people want it to be. A lot of patients get a big tender liver without an abscess. Still, you could do a chest X-ray and see if her right diaphragm is up.'

'Oh. Yessir.'

'And all that stuff about transdiaphragmatic spread and the production of anchovy-paste sputum. . . . It's in all the books, but in a thousand and something cases I saw only a couple with that. It's silly what gets handed down and remembered.' Jean made an I-told-you-so face at Campbell, who would have done it first to her if he had thought of it. 'So we just have to treat her. I wonder if the pharmacy's got bismuth and emetine.'

Again the juniors exchanged looks. Unless someone took charge the old boy would be dusting the leech bottle and bringing out the jar of Dover's Powder. Campbell coughed and said something tactful about some quite encouraging recent reports of the use of metronidazole in this condition.

'Metronidazole? Isn't that something they use over in V.D.?'

'Yessir. It's effective against trichomonas.'

'And against Entamoeba Histolytica?'

'Yessir.'

'When did you see that?'

'Recently, sir,' said Campbell. 'Very recently.' Meaning two or three years ago.

'Oh well. Maybe we could try that. That's interesting. No reason why it shouldn't work of course. Both organisms are protozoans. That's very interesting. . . . Could you find me a reference?'

'Yessir.'

'I published a few papers on this disease myself, you know.' He disappeared and came back a few minutes later with a yellowing reprint, from a military medical journal, of a paper by Major H. J. S. Creech, RAMC. 'They got that wrong you know. I was a lieutenant-colonel when I wrote that. They always get something wrong. All the journals. Anyway, you can borrow that, if you're interested. Just give it back to my secretary when you've finished with it. Good afternoon.'

He disappeared again, leaving Campbell and Jean alone in the duty room.

'He enjoyed that,' said Campbell.

'So did you.'

'Didn't you?'

'Yes, I did. I think he likes medicine, but there are usually too many people around for him to actually get doing any.'

'He seemed all right. Clinically I mean. Except for recent advances in the treatment of amoebiasis.'

'I thought you did that quite tactfully.'

'Thank you.'

'Considering.'

'Thank you very much.'

'And I've still got to write her up.'

'Yes. You do that and I'll add a smug progress note saying that the consultant in administrative charge agrees with our diagnosis.' She made a face. 'And then we can go across the road and drink the health of Mrs Alexander's amoeba.'

'All right. But don't make me drunk, because I'm on duty tonight.'

'I promise. Oh, while I remember, will you just check Theresa's blood.' Campbell had forgotten how infuriating to a houseman were remarks from superiors prefaced 'while I remember'. 'Platelets, white count, that sort of thing.'

'Why?'

'Just in case what's happening to her scalp is happening to her marrow too.'

Jean stopped writing and looked up, serious and beautiful. 'Gosh. Agranulocytosis. I should have thought of that.'

'There's nothing to suggest it clinically, is there?'

'Mouth ulcers, bruising, that sort of thing?'

'Yes.'

'Not that I know of. I'll check again this evening.'

'And bloods tomorrow?'

'Yessir.'

'See you across there at five.'

She smiled a despairing-houseman smile. 'I've still got heaps to do. Say ten past.'

Campbell reached the pub at three minutes past five. Hadden was there already, halfway down a pint.

'Hello, lad. You must think I've been trying to avoid you.'

'No. Why?'

'Oh. After Ma Watters'. I owe you a fiver.'

'Do you? That's nice.'

'So does Baird-Brown. I'll give you a cheque for both and waylay the Blessed Anthony myself.'

'Thanks. . . . That was a good evening.'

'They're a funny old pair.'

Campbell told Hadden a little about the girl who was going to join them, including the odd, late item about Creech knowing her father.

'Oh, that's very Edinburgh,' said Hadden. 'If Jesus Christ arrived in his glory at the General Assembly of the Church of Scotland, some silly bugger would get up and say, "Reverend Moderator, fathers and brethren, it might be apposite to point out to our distinguished visitor, whose remarks we are looking forward very much to hearing, that we knew his father." What was her maiden name?'

'I don't know.'

'Was he in medicine?'

'I don't know. I suppose so.'

Jean came in and Campbell introduced Hadden and went for a second pint for himself and Hadden, and one half of one pint of cider for Jean, whose anti-alcoholism apparently did not exclude token participation. As soon as Campbell sat down she said, 'David, I had another look at Theresa. She's got a sore throat with nothing to show for it, and nasty-looking fresh bruising over both shins. She didn't think she'd bumped them on anything.'

'Anything else?'

'Her hair. It really is awful. She's got a bit of a bald patch now.'

'Oh?' Campbell outlined the case to Hadden, who for some reason that Campbell had never fathomed, knew far more medicine than most surgeons, and for that matter than a lot of physicians.

'Sounds grim. I'd put my money on the wonder drug. Even if nothing else like it has been reported.'

'It's so new. . . .'

'Sometimes people aren't very forthcoming about the nasty things their patent potions do to patients. Remember thalidomide.' He made it sound like the rallying cry of a militant anti-new-drugs movement. 'And marrow depression with bruising, sore throat and anaemia lighting the way to dusty death is one of the commoner patterns of drug-induced disaster. Cheers.'

'Thanks,' said Campbell. 'Jean, I'll come over later. I was going to do a death summary for the GP on Mrs Innes this evening anyway. While I'm across I'll have a look at Theresa too.'

'And you could stop the magic pills,' said Hadden, adding, 'if I might make so bold as to suggest it. How's her ulcer anyway?'

Jean and Campbell looked at each other and Campbell said, 'We're not all that sure she's got one,' and Jean said, 'She just had funny pains that went away.'

'So she'll be another miracle cure chalked up by Edinburgh's new wonder drug. If she lives.'

It was after eight before Campbell left the pub. Hadden was going back across to the Institute too, to cast an eye over his patients from that morning's list before he went home. They stepped out into the last of the evening's sunlight and stood waiting for a break in the traffic. They had been talking and drinking for more than three hours. After Jean had gone, refusing even another half pint of cider, they had lingered on and on. Other people from the Institute, nurses, housemen on call, porters and the like, had come and gone. Bones had rushed in and then joined them carrying a half pint and a pie, eaten and drunk very quickly, and rushed out again to assist with some mishap of cardiac surgery, a valve displacement bleeding uncontrollably who was to be reopened in ten minutes. During his brief manifestation he had commented variously on the beer, the pie, the Theatre Sister's teeth, the staff nurse's tits, his consultant's language, the sloth of the portering service from Blood Transfusion and the patient's chances, evidently slim. Hadden and Campbell had listened and watched as he talked, spluttering crumbs of pie and waving his hands, and had resumed their previous conversation when he left.

Hadden was two years Campbell's senior in the great chain of medical being. He had worked in or near the Institute since qualifying and knew a vast amount about its workings. Within his own chosen specialty of surgery his professional knowledge was large and his grasp of the nuances of behaviour within the surgical tribe was a revelation to Campbell, whose impressions of that clan were simple and unflattering. That aura of mindless violence, most marked among thoracic and orthopaedic surgeons and shading off through belly men and kidney-and-bladder men to the relatively gentlemanly neurosurgeons on the top floor, was, it appeared, only part of the picture. Hadden had talked of them as individuals with interests, not only predictable ones like golf and piping, but some surprising things, like the organ-playing of an apparently bone-headed urologist and the quite unexpected ornithological expertise of Mr Alester Ravelston Orr ('Not by any means just blazing away at anything that flies past on the twelfth of August, as you might imagine.').

Just as he knew more than was expected of him of medicine, Hadden knew a lot about physicians too, and was distinctly suspicious of Rosamund's doings, be they manipulation of research puppets like Campbell or arm's length evaluations of possibly dangerous drugs, so conducted as to make full use of Bill Dempster's manic optimism. 'Drug companies don't give money to pessimists' was a Hadden aphorism that Campbell thought might stick in his mind despite the pint or two prior to his hearing it. Comparing information about Ratho, Bertram, Roddy and others around Creech's unit had also proved interesting. Campbell was aware of having talked of Jean at a length and in a detail disproportionate to any political or tribal significance she might have. Hadden had listened knowingly.

They crossed the road and passed through the great iron gates. Hadden turned right towards the territory of the surgeons, and Campbell leftwards down the hill to the easeful plains of medicine, seeking first the staff toilet next to the research fellows' room.

After a much delayed pee he found to his surprise that he was probably more drunk than he had supposed on first leaving the pub with Hadden. Nonetheless, he felt that a straightforward death summary of an elderly hemiplegic was still well within his competence, and went up to the ward, where he sat down in the duty room with the late Mrs Innes's notes, reading through her simple story. 'Previously well. Sudden onset of left sided weakness. Investigations unremarkable. Recovery slow but sustained over three months. Recurrent cerebro-vascular accident and death.' The nursing notes, as always posthumously included in the back flap of the case folder, told the same story in simpler language and better handwriting. 'Cheerful. Good day. Good night. Settled. Happy with progress. 83rd birthday. Deteriorating. Died.'

Campbell took a blank sheet from Jean's new wooden paper rack and jotted down the dates, events and main findings, with a view to going back to the research fellows' room to dictate it on to a tape. As he finished he remembered Theresa and went into the ward to examine her throat, her bruising and her rapidly advancing hair loss. A nurse on duty gave him an old-fashioned look.

Before he had reached his patient, Jean came down the ward to meet him.

'David, what brings you up here?'

'I thought I'd look at Theresa.' He had not previously realised how hard it was to pronounce that name, with its deceptive initial 'th'. 'I said I would.'

She came close to him, so close that it occurred to him that she might be smelling his breath. 'She's mainly all right. I'll tell you about her.'

Campbell found himself walking with Jean, back out of the ward. They went into the duty room again and she picked up a green case folder labelled Theresa Murgatroyd 010954.

'Let's sit down in Sister's room and I'll tell you all about her.'

'All right.' Campbell felt that he was being fairly firmly managed by his junior staff, but didn't mind because he liked her. Jean sat down opposite him in one of Sister's red plush armchairs. She was leaning forward, with Theresa's case notes on her knees.

'David. . . .'

'What?'

'David, are you all right?'

'Fine. You keep asking that.'

'No. . . . I mean. . . .'

'I'm not drunk or anything. . . .'

'Have you had anything to eat?'

'Not really. We thought we might have pies, but Bones put us off.'

'What? Oh, never mind. . . . I'll get you something. . . . I've written a bit about what's happening to Theresa.' She handed him the case notes and went out.

Campbell liked reading her writing in the same way as he liked listening to her voice; she wrote sensible progress notes clearly, and the latest three instalments in the tale of Theresa Murgatroyd described an unmistakable crisis. One from the morning noted the hair loss, and the things she had told him in the pub were detailed in a paragraph marked '5 p.m.' in the margin. That one ended 'Blood taken for emergency haemoglobin, white count and platelets'. The blood taken at five counted for extra points. Another, marked '8 p.m.' described further bruising. Once more Jean had proved a better houseman than Campbell had anticipated.

With slow, drunken precision Campbell put together the facts of the case from his previous knowledge and recent details supplied by Jean, and then went on to consider the various possibilities now facing the patient, mainly on the basis of information arising from the discussion in the pub with Hadden. The most likely diagnosis was, as Hadden had said, a drug-induced suppression of bone marrow, which carried a triple threat to life. The most immediate arose from a tendency to bruise and bleed resulting from the absence of the platelets, whose main function was to trigger off the sealing of damaged blood vessels and the clotting of blood. Next came the diminished resistance to infection caused by the loss of the white blood cells, and last but none the less threatening was the intractable anaemia which loss of red blood cell production invariably heralded. These three problems might arise independently or in combination. It was unlikely that she had yet developed a significant anaemia, but Campbell very much wanted to know the results of the five o'clock white cell and platelet counts.

Jean came back with a tray of tea and toast and a jar of Marmite. 'There weren't any eggs.'

'What?'

'I was going to make you scrambled eggs.'

'That would have been nice.'

'This'll have to do.'

'Thanks. It's great. . . . What was Theresa's five o'clock platelet count?'

'Under twenty thousand.'

'Bloody hell.' The normal was between a hundred thousand and a quarter million. 'And the white count?'

'Two thousand.' That too was well below normal.

'She needs platelets.'

'I've ordered them. . . .'

'Good.'

'That's what we're waiting for.'

'And a drip up.'

'That's what I was doing when you came in.'

'How's the bruising?'

'Spreading a bit. Some on her thighs and arms too now.'

'Maybe I should see it.'

'There's no need, David. I think I'm coping. Have some Marmite.'

'What about telling someone. I mean apart from me. Like Rosamund.'

'I thought I'd ring her up when we'd actually got the platelets going in.'

'You're a star housegirl.'

'I'm not really. . . . But I'm glad I didn't have that other half pint.'

Toast made by Jean was, naturally, perfect. Campbell sat and ate the toast and drank the tea. Jean had tea only. Dusk fell outside, and neither moved to switch on the light in Sister's room. They sat for a long time in one of their companionable silences and once more Campbell felt himself being swept from present harsh reality on a great drunken sentimental tide of yearning for her. Being with her, even when he was half-drunk, being looked after by her, and, he had to admit, perhaps being protected by her from possible indiscretion, seemed the most worthwhile things that had happened to him that day, a glimpse almost of a better, higher life. Her calm rationality, her competence and concern reminded him of an idealism he had had once about medicine, an idealism perhaps still persisting somewhere, though ignored and neglected since practically the beginning of his own time as a houseman.

She leaned towards him to pour more tea, and the smell of her hair burst once again into his awareness. He drew breath sharply and she looked up, her face close in the dusk. Campbell sat helpless, stunned by beer and tea and toast and Marmite and the smell of Jean's hair and by Jean herself, close and caring. Her deep grey-blue eyes, large in the dusk, searched his unresisting face.

There was a knock at the door and a young student nurse put her head round it, peering as though puzzled to find two doctors sitting thus in a darkening room. She switched on the light and Campbell blinked. When he opened his eyes the world was different, and as it had been before.

'The porter's here with some stuff from BTS. He said you said it was urgent, Dr Moray.'

'Thanks, nurse.' Jean got up and Campbell did too. 'It'll be the platelet concentration. I'll see to it.'

'Jean, I'm going to ring Bill. It's his thing and he ought to know about it.'

'Fine. And I'll ring Rosamund when I've put this up on Theresa.'

'Okay.'

She went off into the ward and Campbell rang Bill Dempster, who seemed remarkably unconcerned. 'Well, if she's getting platelets and you're watching her white count and her haemoglobin there's not much more you can do. I suppose it might be the new drug. But as you know there are hundreds of causes of marrow suppression and anyway in at least half the cases no cause is found. I think the spontaneous kind might even be commoner in mongols. I seem to remember having read something about that somewhere.'

'Anyway, we've stopped the KM stuff.'

'Fair enough. But you know aspirin can cause it. And paracetamol. Has she had either of those in the last six weeks?'

'Who hasn't?'

'Exactly. So you can't just rush in and incriminate KM 1103. It's a very promising drug and must be given a fair chance. It might even put the surgeons right out of the ulcer business.'

'So I've heard.'

'Oh, and another thing. I shouldn't go into too many details with the relatives until you've discussed it fully with Rosamund.'

'There aren't any relatives.'

'Fine. Any other problems?'

'I think we're coping.'

'Yes, Jean's very good, isn't she?'

'Yes. Thanks, Bill. Goodnight.'

Jean was waiting when Campbell put the phone down. 'The platelets are going in now. I'll ring Rosamund.'

A minute later she rejoined him in the duty room. 'Rosamund didn't seem too bothered.'

'Neither did Bill. He said we'd done everything reasonable, and anyway it might not be his KM stuff that was doing it. But I said we're still stopping it.'

'Gosh.' Jean put her hand up to her mouth. 'I forgot that.' She looked at her watch. 'There's still time to stop her ten o'clock dose. If I'd been on the ball we could have stopped it before the six o'clock one.'

'I don't think one tablet's going to make an awful lot of difference.'

'Oh, I feel awful about that. I made a mental note as soon as your friend Mr Hadden mentioned it in the pub.'

'Don't worry about it. You're not awful. Not at all. You're fine. You really are.'

'Am I?' Jean was quiet and thoughtful, then pulled her white coat round herself tightly in a way that meant she was about to go. There was a piece of paper with Campbell's writing on it lying on the desk. He picked it up. It was the brief life of Mrs Innes, awaiting dictation. He folded it and put it in his inside pocket.

'I'd better go before the night staff smell my breath,' said Campbell. 'Ring me at the flat if there are any more problems overnight. . . . Thanks for the toast and things.'

'My pleasure. Goodnight, David.'

'Goodnight, Jean.'

Campbell walked across the park, towards his flat where Joan was waiting, through the warm summer night, thinking of Jean and still a little bit drunk. Halfway across he got a nasty surprise. Someone had removed the warning lamps where the labourers had been working, and he only narrowly avoided falling down the hole, which was now six feet deep.

Next morning Theresa was bald. There was not a single hair left on her head, which was small, shining, dome-shaped and radiantly white. Even her eyebrows were thin. Campbell had never seen a bald mongol before and her appearance was intriguing as well as rather disturbing. Her red eyes and pinkish, crowded features looked even stranger under their new superstructure. She was very upset and had spent a lot of the morning with her head buried amid pillows and blankets. Jean was also somewhat distressed at this development, but with characteristic efficiency had already started to organise a wig, with the help of the cancer chemotherapy people, whose patients quite regularly went bald on treatment.

As a result of Jean's evening phone call, Rosamund had made one of her rare visits to the ward and looked briefly at Theresa's head, throat and bruising, by now even more extensive, and talked with her junior staff. Campbell was given the delicate task of ringing the priest from St Cuthbert's. 'Just say it's not uncommon in mongols. . . . No. Just say it's not uncommon in mongols with ulcers.' While she was talking he got a distinct impression that he was somehow meant to have made this phone call without having been told, though he could clearly remember the conversation in which she had said she would keep the priest informed personally. She also had views on the wig proposed by Jean. 'Nothing too striking. No honey tresses. Simple, short and plain, please. Absurdity must be avoided.' As she left the ward she stopped opposite an empty cubicle, one of two normally reserved for patients who were either disturbed, distinguished or moribund. 'And it might be an idea to pop her in there for a little while, staff. Her appearance is a little strange, certainly for the time being. She'll probably appreciate the privacy too. And her future, moreover, might be . . . uncertain.'

She left and Jean and Campbell went on with their ward round, looking at both Creech's and Rosamund's patients. Mrs Alexander, after one day on metronidazole, said she felt better already. Her temperature had dropped a little and her abdomen was less tender. She thanked Campbell for his efforts, so profusely that he wondered if he were about to displace the contemptible Ratho in her pantheon of her medical attendants.

Mrs Herron was looking expectantly at them as they came near her bed. The doctors, perhaps out of earshot, conversed.

'What's happening here, Jean?'

'Oh. Didn't you see the note for you from Rosamund?'

'No.'

'She says we still haven't completely excluded simple biliary obstruction.'

'What?'

'Gallstones.'

'Gallstones?'

'She told me yesterday that in a few cases reported in the literature a picture just like primary biliary cirrhosis was caused by chronic obstruction of the common bile duct, usually by stone.'

'That must be very rare.'

'She says it is, but because it's treatable we've got to exclude it.'

'So what's happening?'

'She's spoken to someone called Ravelston Orr.'

'Oh, God.'

'What?'

'That should be interesting. She wants him to explore the common bile duct?'

'Yes.'

'When's that to be done?'

'Well, that's what you're supposed to find out, or fix up, or whatever you do. And something about arranging any pre-op clotting screen and what they want her cross-matched for. She gave me a little note I put on your desk in the research fellows' room.'

'I haven't looked there this morning yet.'

'Anyway that's what's happening. . . . Is he dangerous?'

'Well, he's . . . interesting. I did a housejob there. We had our moments. For myself, I wouldn't go near him for an ingrown toenail, if I had one.'

Campbell had felt sorry for Mrs Herron even before this latest turn in her fortunes. In many ways she was an ideal patient; polite, grateful and intelligent enough to talk to. She had a bad disease and now to complicate matters she was down for a highly speculative operation at the hands of a surgeon of proverbial unpredictability.

'So what's happening?' said Mrs Herron.

'Well,' said Campbell, 'I've got some good news for you. . . . Dr Fyvie has arranged for you to have an operation that gives a good chance of clearing things up once and for all.' After he had said it, he realised his last phrase had a perhaps unnecessarily eschatological flavour to it. 'To look at the biliary passages out of the liver and see if they can be cleared.'

'What's he like?'

'Who?'

'The surgeon who'll be doing the operation.'

Campbell smiled professionally. 'A scholar and a gentleman. He's quite famous too.' There was no point at all in saying what he was famous for.

Mrs Herron smiled too. 'When will it be?'

'I'm just going over to make the arrangements shortly. We'll let you know as soon as anything's fixed up.'

Campbell and Jean went for coffee, and talked about the technicalities of Theresa's various problems. They were colleagues again, as if the near-intimacy of the previous night had never been. For the first time between them, silence was awkward.

Eventually Bertram came in, poured himself a coffee and flopped down in a chair. 'I hate Tuesdays. Nearly as much as Mondays.'

'What's wrong?' said Jean.

'I'm doing a damn silly experiment I never believe in till Wednesdays. And by then it's too late to set it up before Friday. And I was just thinking that if I were in practice I'd just be stretching my legs on a few house calls or sitting reading the BMA pamphlet on how to get extra money for sitting reading pamphlets, or polishing the Volvo, maybe, if it was a nice day.'

Bertram's departure for general practice had been imminent as long as Campbell had known him. His discontent in academic medicine was chronic and invariably briefly exacerbated when attractive partnerships in the district fell vacant. He suffered agonies when he was phoned up, as happened from time to time, by ex-classmates who felt his physicianly acumen would add lustre to their practices. But he stayed around, climbing slowly up the ladder, growing publications over the years, inexorably, like barnacles, despite his declared distaste for research. He was the unit factotum and was reported to have the ear of the senior consultant. His recent small patronage of Campbell had given that acolyte the feeling that he too was a subscriber, however lowly, to the intricate system of nods, mentions and quiet words that kept Edinburgh medicine going on down the years to its own entire satisfaction.

He turned on Campbell. 'Now, young David, what are you going to talk about at the unit meeting?'

'What?'

'Don't try that "Who me?" stuff with me, Campbell. Friday. You're on second.'

'Doing what?'

'An interesting case?' Bertram suggested.

'I don't have any.'

'You must have. You've got a dozen beds. What's in the ward?'

'A bald mongol?' Jean made a face.

'What?'

'Theresa Murgatroyd's hair all fell out last night. Bill's drug.'

'That's a bit sick. Try again.'

'A case of primary biliary cirrhosis that might might just might turn out to be a case of gallstones.'

'Mmm. It might not.'

'That's what we thought.'

'Come on, lad. What else have you got?'

'What about Mrs Alexander?' said Jean.

'What's she got?' said Bertram.

'Amoebiasis,' said Campbell, trying to make it sound like 'flu.

'Amoebiasis!' Bertram whooped. 'The boss's favourite disease. Campbell, you'll be made an honorary consultant and we'll all have to call you sir. Where on earth did you find that?'

'In a clinic.'

'Get away. Just a new patient? Fresh in off the street?'

'No. A follow up.'

'A follow up? Fantastic. What was she being followed up as?'

'Ulcerative colitis.'

'Great! What clinic?'

'The Tuesday colitics.'

'Ratho's?'

'Yes.'

'That sounds like an interesting case, young Campbell. You're on second. Friday afternoon.'

'She's pretty straightforward really. No abscess. No spread. Routine stuff getting better on the standard treatment.'

'Come on, young Campbell. You're not going to get out of a case presentation as easily as that.'

'No, I didn't mean that. I just meant why her. There's a lot to that cirrhosis woman Herron. She had itching and everything. Good signs. And we might have a final answer by Friday afternoon.'

'No,' said Bertram. 'From the sound of things your amoebiasis is a much more interesting case.'

Jean went back to the ward and Campbell and Bertram sat for a while, discussing cases on the ward at first then drifting via Theresa towards gossip. Bertram thought that Bill Dempster should be told about the recent events in Theresa's life. Campbell complained that he wasn't the easiest of people to find.

'No,' said Bertram. 'He's got a lot on his plate.'

'His commitments,' said Campbell.

'His numerous commitments.'

'Here and at the Southern.'

'And down in Transfusion.'

'And over in the library.'

'And of course he gets called away for specimens from operations here and there.'

'And he manages a bit of fishing.' Campbell recalled Jean's story.

'And the occasional GP surgery.'

'Really?'

'Oh, yes. He once managed a whole week's locum without taking leave from here.'

'And his family.'

'And his family problems,' said Bertram. Campbell remembered that the unit secretary had used the same phrase in relation to Bill.

'Really?'

'Seen out for a quiet evening's drive in the country with one of them the other day.'

'Really?'

'Yes.' Bertram got up. 'So that's on for Friday. Mrs whatever. The amoeba lady. Will you be having some slides made up?'

Having slides made up for teaching and case presentations was another harmless pastime, widely practised within the unit, that Campbell had not yet got round to. 'Maybe. If I can find the time. There's quite a lot just now that I have to get on with.'

Since he had read the *Guardian* early Campbell had to find something to do until it was time for lunch. He did not relish the prospect of starting work on the 5000-word synopsis for Rosamund of his territory of research and his future plans within it. Snodgrass had failed, both as a scientist and as a prose stylist, to re-excite Campbell's enthusiasm since his first dip into the book down in ICU. An amble down the surgical corridor and perhaps a look into one or two of the operating theatres on the off chance that some patient might just have been relieved of all or part of his colon seemed the most undemanding way to fill the hour or so and still call it work. As he walked up to the surgical side of the hospital he stopped at the shop and bought a *Scotsman* for its crossword.

In the operating theatre observation gallery with the most comfortable seating Jocasta Smith was reading a reprint from a learned journal. There was a row of glass specimen bottles on the bench beside her.

'David!'

'Hello, Dr Smith.'

'Jo,' she said as though mildly rebuking him. 'I was just about to phone you, David. As soon as I got my bit of this breast that's just coming up.'

'Were you?'

'Yes. I've got you the most super bit of colon. I hope it'll be enough. It's in isotonic saline just as you said.' She reached out to the bench behind and handed Campbell a wide-mouthed glass jar in which a grey hank of gut lay curled in two inches of saline, like an obscure and long-dead sea creature.

'Oh. . . . Thanks. Thanks very much.'

'I expect you've done heaps by now. But I got you that bit anyway. I'm sure if it's anything like my project every little helps.'

'Yes. . . . Yes. . .?'

Campbell thanked her again, folded up his *Scotsman*, took the jar and left. He walked through the hospital towards the vitamin assay lab carrying his specimens almost proudly. He had made a serious start in research.

The vitamin assay laboratory was in a semi-basement under a ground-floor ward in the lowest part of the hospital. Together with a small office and a consulting room, it had been the empire of a notoriously eccentric consultant physician whose enthusiasm for vitamins in diagnosis and treatment, though rooted in the conventional medicine of the time of his training, had latterly become a great embarrassment to his colleagues, and this quiet suite of rooms had been as much an exile as anything else. On his retirement it had passed, as a result of some fast and nasty committee work, into the growing domain of Rosamund Fyvie, who had not, prior to this coup, been particularly interested in vitamins. Campbell, as Rosamund's white hope in the vitamin field, had been given to understand that, in return for diligence and a decent yardage of published papers, one day all this would be his. Already he had sensed his feudal status in relation to it, his responsibility for it to Rosamund, though he had not as yet created any work for it to do.

When he took his specimen down, Lorna, the technician, was cleaning out a cupboard. Ancient dusty mahogany boxes of forgotten clinical instruments saw the light for the first time in decades. She was kneeling over a brass microscope like a miniature antique howitzer. She looked up.

'Oh. It's you. Have you got something for me to assay?'

'I think so. Quite a good bit of colon.'

'Good. I was getting bored with cupboards.' She stood up. She not only sounded nicer than the average lab technician, she smelled nicer too. She was about five foot six, with smooth short very dark hair and deep brown eyes. Among other things about her, Campbell had noted on his Monday morning reconnaissance, she was probably in her late twenties, and married. Their conversation on Monday had been factual and professional, concerning methods and materials, and she had given Campbell a copy of Rosamund's draft protocol for the experiment, which he had taken away and not read. Even at their first meeting Campbell had wondered if a certain liveliness displayed in that arid exchange might later, in the course of long afternoons slaving together over the hot assay specimens, transform itself into something more substantial. He had also wondered, perhaps on the basis of experience obtained elsewhere, if married women sometimes did things like that in order to promote a sort of platonic amelioration of working relationships, especially with male superiors.

'I'm afraid I left my protocol up in the research fellows' room.'

'That's all right. I've got lots. And I practically know it off by heart anyway. I've had nothing to do but cupboards and read it since I started. . . . Your bit begins with weighing out aliquots of mucosa and disaggregating them with collagenase.'

'Does it?' said Campbell. She looked at him quizzically.

Like two rather new cooks in an unfamiliar kitchen, Campbell and his technician muddled through, referring frequently to the protocol. The first part of the method was frankly messy. Campbell opened the tube of gut and cut it into strips, then scraped the mucosal lining from the muscular outer coat of the specimen. Then Lorna weighed out two-gram portions into a row of beakers and added twenty mils of the collagenase solution, using a pipette with a familiar expertise that Campbell could not have emulated.

'Half an hour's incubation with that then shake it all up with glass beads.'

'You've been practising,' said Campbell.

'Not really. Just read it a few times. How about some coffee?'

Perhaps there were consolations to be found in the cloistered life of medical research. While an enzyme incubated at thirty-seven degrees centigrade did your work for you, fragmenting a specimen in which you hoped eventually to measure vitamin concentrations, you sat and had coffee with a reasonably attractive girl who was still sufficiently unfamiliar to be interesting. Over coffee Campbell interrogated her gently about routine things, such as where she had trained, her last job, what she thought of Rosamund, and how she felt about the project in which they were both involved. On that last issue, she was well-informed but non-committal, and Campbell realised an important difference between technical and professional staff in medical research. Doctors were expected, however haltingly, to believe in it; technicians just did it.

Campbell's exploration of this was cut short by a buzzing sound from the incubator. Lorna opened it and took out the beakers.

'What do we do now?'

'Smash up the soup with glass beads. Gently.'

She transferred the specimens to a row of test tubes, and added into each a few glass beads. On the bench was an odd little machine with a rubber head which vibrated when she switched it on. She held each test tube in turn against the rubber for a few seconds and the glass beads rattled inside.

'That's clever.'

'Standard technique. Then centrifuge them with xylol. But if it's okay with you, can we do that after lunch?'

'Fine by me. I've got some out-patients in the early afternoon. Can we start again about three?'

'Okay. Is it all right if I take an extra half hour over lunch?'

No one had ever made such a request to Campbell before. He agreed.

'Thanks.'

They put the specimens in their test tubes in a wooden rack on the bench and left the lab together. Campbell went up to the research fellows' room to hang up his white coat and get his jacket, feeling once more that life in research might not be quite as deadly as anticipated.

On the way to lunch he looked into the female ward. Jean was not around. As he left the priest from St Cuthbert's, Theresa's protector, rushed past on his way out. He turned and said to Campbell over his shoulder, 'Must fly. I see you've shifted her. She might like the privacy but I'm not so sure. Kind of you anyway. She's asleep and I didn't want to waken her. Nice of you to think of a wig. Her own hair never was up to much.' Campbell walked quickly after him and started to speak. 'Must fly,' said the priest again, disappearing down the stairs, his green socks twinkling beneath his trouser bottoms at every step.

There was ample time before Ratho's Tuesday colitis clinic, so Campbell left the Institute with the intention of going for a short walk before lunch. Heavy grey and white clouds, the first in days and days of unblemished summer were gathering over the hills to the south. As he had no coat he abandoned the idea of a walk and went instead to the pub across the road, where he drank two pints of beer fairly quickly on his own, wondering if he was likely to find himself doing this sort of thing often.

In the Institute once more he queued behind a female consultant physician who, when they got to the counter, proved to be so lacking, either by nature or the conditioning of her specialty, in the ability to take decisions that several minutes passed before she made up her mind between the steamed and the baked fish. Campbell pushed past, to her muttered rebuke, and only afterwards reflected that she might one day be found on a selection committee interviewing him for a job, or even examining for the higher qualification he had not yet got round to thinking seriously about.

He ate alone, and then had coffee on the lawn by himself, watching the huge banks of cumulo-nimbus towering above the Pentlands. The afternoon was hot and the air still and heavy. The people nearby on the lawn, and the hospital around it, seemed irksome and oppressive. Having eaten too much too quickly on top of unaccustomed lunchtime beer, he sat long after he had finished his coffee, in a state of simmering physical and mental discomfort, contemplating with disgust the prospect of Ratho's Tuesday clinic, and wondering what had happened to Jean.

There were only two patients at the clinic, both dull and neither with amoebiasis. One had brought a large and revolting collection of wax cartons which, it was said, Dr Ratho had particularly requested. There was nothing in the notes about it, and as soon as the patient had gone Campbell consigned them to the waste paper basket. The clinic was finished by half past two: he dictated the letters straight away and, having found his notes for the death summary on Mrs Innes, added that in to the same tape.

Lorna was sitting polishing the old brass microscope when Campbell went back to the lab to resume his first vitamin assay. To have a decorative and obsolete piece of equipment round the place as a paperweight or conversation piece or whatever seemed a nice idea, and Campbell noted it in her favour. She looked round, and as she did so, seemed to Campbell nervous and preoccupied.

'Oh, hello.'

'Hello.' Campbell glanced round for his five specimens. 'Have you just gone straight on and done the xylol extractions already?'

She looked blank. 'The specimens from this morning,' he prompted her.

'Oh, Christ.' She put both hands up to her face so that Campbell could not see it at all, and kept on saying, 'Oh, Christ. Oh, Christ.'

'What's happened,' said Campbell, 'to my life's work?'

'I'm so sorry. . . . Oh, Christ. . . . How could I have been so idiotic?' On the bench where the specimens had been there was no rack, no tubes, no specimens.

'What have you done with them?'

She took her hands down from her face, now suffused and

blank. 'You'll never believe what I've done.'

'Try me,' said Campbell, fearing the worst.

'I came in after lunchtime . . . and just c . . . cleared up.'

'Cleared up those specimens?'

'Just poured them down the sink and washed the test tubes. Without thinking about it.'

'Oh, Christ,' said Campbell in his turn. 'What were you thinking about? Bloody hell. . . . It's not as if it's the culmination of years of labour like poor Newton and his bloody dog knocking over the candle and all that. But it's a nuisance. First steps in research and all that.'

She sat down on a lab stool and began to cry. 'Oh, I'm sorry. It was idiotic of me I know. Oh, Christ. I don't know what I was thinking about.' She pulled a handful of tissues from a blue box and sniffed.

'Sorry,' said Campbell. 'I didn't mean to go on about it like that. It's happened. I'll get another bit tomorrow, I suppose.'

She sat opposite him, with her back to the window, weeping as if she had decided to go at it for a while. 'I went to see Sam today. He's in hospital. . . . And. . . .'

'Your husband?'

'No, my kid . . . My husband poked off six months ago.' She wept a bit more.

Campbell, who had precipitated the outburst, felt like a motorist who had knocked over a nun and then discovered she had not only a caliper but a hearing aid as well. 'Look, I'd no idea. . . . I'm sorry. Forget about those specimen things. . . . Take the afternoon off.'

'What's the point? Oh, everything's just been so bloody for the last four days. And we were just getting . . . organised.'

'What's wrong with him?'

'Chest,' she sniffed. 'Croup. Probably RSV.'

'People usually get better from that.'

'Oh, yes. He's not going to die or anything. But he's just so pathetic, lying in an oxygen thing wanting to be cuddled.' Her crying, which had subsided a little, regained its initial intensity. Campbell put a gingerly hand on her shoulders and said, 'Have some tea or coffee or something.'

This precipitated a further burst of weeping. She put a hand on his, tense and urgent, and Campbell realised perhaps with belated surprise that it was not only Sam in his oxygen tent who wanted to be cuddled. He moved closer and she stood up, so close that her head was on his shoulder. She put her arms round him and sobbed against him, rocking to and fro, and saying 'Oh, Christ' and sniffing. Campbell remembered the couch in the consulting room next door.

'Christ, I needed that,' said Lorna. Their lab coats lay in an intimate heap on the floor. Lorna's light summer dress was crumpled under her armpits and Campbell was in a state of partial undress commonly associated with shady lanes and police courts. He kissed her.

'You don't have to kiss me as well, but thanks,' she said. She had stopped crying. Her eyes were red but she looked happier. 'How about climbing off and getting me some paper hankies?'

Campbell complied, kissing her first to maintain the social ambience. She laughed and said, 'You're sweet.'

He came back with a big handful. She said, 'That should be enough,' and took them. Campbell picked up the two lab coats from the floor. She stood up and shook down her dress, stooped and picked up her pants, all in one graceful movement. 'Now let's have that coffee you mentioned.'

Campbell met Hadden in the pub at five. As they sat drinking Jocasta Smith came in with a group of junior doctors from the professorial surgical unit. Campbell remembered his indebtedness to her. She smiled at him as she passed, and then kept looking at him from the surgical table at the other side of the pub. When her group began to break up shortly after six she came over towards Hadden and Campbell. Campbell thanked her for the specimen without telling her what had happened to it or how much it had done for staff morale in the lab, introduced Hadden to her and asked her if she would like to join them for a drink. She had a whisky.

Conversation in the trio was hard going. Campbell had the impression that Jocasta was directing most of her attention to him rather than to Hadden. Her contributions were her usual mixture of unit gossip and what the professor thought, together with a slightly wet-lipped enthusiasm for her own project, the breast thing that might have something to do with cancer. They had a few more drinks and Campbell decided she had nice eyes and her skin was not as dreadful as he had thought. While she was in the loo Hadden said, 'Take care, lad.'

'What about?'

'Or something beautiful might happen to you.'

'With her?' Campbell considered it, trying to balance the thought of her bosom against the sound of her voice.

'Oh, I think so,' said Hadden. 'It could easily turn out to be the greatest breakthrough since lunchtime.'

'Hmm. It might.'

Two hours later, after an Indian meal and a slow walk back to the flat, Campbell tested the hypothesis on the lounge carpet, amid Bones' railway track and GWR rolling stock. She was awkward and a bit smelly. He was drunk and got carried away and afterwards Jocasta asked him, 'Have you got another girl-friend, David? Called Jean?'

FOUR

'Hello.'

'Hello.'

'Aren't you supposed to be at Rosamund's Wednesday meeting?'

'Aren't you?'

'I suppose so, but knowing you're not there either makes me feel better about it. . . . Are you off?'

'Sort of. I thought I'd do some reading at the flat.' Campbell brandished Snodgrass's solid red monograph like a very large passport. 'And I seem to have been to too many clinical meetings in the last week. They're all beginning to sound the same.'

'I know what you mean.' Jean was a bit breathless, having run a couple of hundred yards over the grass to join Campbell on his way across the park. He had heard her voice calling his name, and turned to see her running towards him from the railings of the Institute, her hair flying and her legs going beautifully, all functional elegance, like a wildlife filmclip.

'How did you get out?' Campbell nodded towards the apparently impenetrable expanse of railing separating the Institute from the park.

'There's a short cut. A broken bit in the railings just near Haematology. I usually come that way and across the grass, if it's dry.'

They walked together along the path and past the labourers, who were all stripped to the waist, as much sunning themselves as working in and around their pit with various pieces of pipe. One of them, from below ground level, whistled at Jean, who pretended, rather obviously, not to have noticed.

'Super day, isn't it?'

'Shame to work. Better to be off.'

'Mmmm. But I'll sort of work. Read about vitamins out on the roof. . . . We've got a flat sunny bit.'

'Lucky you. We haven't.'

'You live in Marchmont too?'

'Yes. . . . How are the assays going?'

'Stuck just now. Technician's off. Started, though.'

'Sick?'

'Not her. Her kid.'

'What's the matter?'

'RSV.'

'Poor thing.'

Campbell had wondered about Jean and children. They had talked about medical women and families: sometimes she sounded as if she thought that kids were something that happened to other people, and sometimes as if they were the common lot to be merely tolerated, like going to the dentist.

'He'll live. She got him out early, to look after him at home.'

'Is she any good?'

'Seems okay. Bright.'

'That must help your research.' Campbell wondered if she were being snide. If he had said something like that, it would have been. He looked round at her, and decided it wasn't.

She was wearing a sleeveless striped summer dress with a big open neckline. The bits of her he couldn't see were tantalisingly imaginable, with a faint line across her hips marking the top of her pants. Her waist, slim and within easy reach to his right as they walked, was too lovely and too close for comfort. He swopped Snodgrass from his left hand to his right as an aid to self-discipline and an obstacle to perhaps disastrously inappropriate initiative. That seemed to make her walk closer.

She turned towards him and said, almost as if it were a secret of great mutual concern that she had just heard, 'Theresa's platelet count's up a bit today.'

'Good. But isn't that mainly because we're giving her so many of them?'

'Maybe.'

They walked on. Campbell knew that they would talk about something else to do with work and the ward quite soon, but was for the moment happy simply to walk beside her in the sun on a tree-lined path which led diagonally across the park from the Institute towards the sloping clutter of genteel tenements in which, it appeared, they both lived.

'Mrs Herron's worried about the operation,' said Jean.

'Friday?'

'Friday morning. That Orr man. Your old chief.'

'Yes. I thought I might go over and see what they find.' Campbell just stopped himself saying 'to save the trouble of going to the post mortem'.

'I might go too, if there's time.' A tentative platonic bloody date. 'I saw Mr Herron. Yesterday while you were doing your vitamins. He's not really in touch at all. He sort of thinks because she's going for an operation she's going to get better quicker. Talking about their holiday again.'

'That's the idea though. Rosamund thinks it might just be a stone.'

'D'you think it is?'

'I hope it is.'

'But think it won't be.'

'Right. Rosamund just hopes too. I don't think she really thinks it is. It might just be one of her games.'

'Games?'

'With surgeons. You give them a case like that. Someone they can either refuse or go into against the odds and maybe kill. And you know how surgeons think. Either way the physician looks clever.'

'That's nasty. . . . Don't they get on?'

'Rosamund and Alester?'

'Yes.'

'I've heard they pretend to. And fight on committees.'

They came to the end of the path, where a crumbling arch of whales' jawbones commemorating a knitwear exhibition in 1886 marked the limit of the park. They stopped before crossing the road beyond. Jean turned and looked closely at Campbell, her eyes half-closed against the sun.

'David?'

'What?'

'Would you like to come up for some tea?'

'Y . . . yes. Thanks.'

'What about your vitamins?'

'I've got a whole year to contemplate their mysteries.'

'I'm just up here.' She pointed up the hill to the right. Campbell noted another interesting example of choice of pronoun for his proposed study.

As they crossed the road, he was struck by a sense of possible impending enormity. He felt like a soldier thinking about volunteering for a parachute course and then being told suddenly that he was to be dropped into enemy territory that night. Jean went on talking casually about one of their patients, as if she were very much in the habit of having admirers up casually for tea on her afternoons off. They turned into a small sunlit square, and Jean went silent too.

'This is it. . . . We're two floors up.' The newest nameplate beside the main door was the one indicating the second-floor left-hand flat. It was plastic, shiny and black, and said 'J. Moray'. The stone stairway was cool and after the bright afternoon light of the square, gloomy and awkward to a stranger. Jean went ahead, and Campbell followed her pale legs up two flights of stairs.

She produced a key, and as she put it to the door there was a deafening noise from within, a horrible cacophony of barking, the sound of a large and very excited dog. The barking changed to a kind of ecstatic howl accompanied by frantic scratching on the other side of the door.

'I've got a dog,' said Jean, pushing the door open. A creamy-golden Labrador, full-grown but still young, burst out on to the landing, sniffing excitedly around them, whipping its tail against their legs and making eager whimpering noises. Jean put a hand down towards it, which it licked affectionately. 'You don't mind dogs, do you, David?'

'No.'

'She's called Sally. She's nice but a bit stupid. Inside, Sally.'

Campbell followed them into a standard small Marchmont flat, one of hundreds in the immediate vicinity, variously occupied by students, young professionals and decaying spinsters and widows. The decor was safe rather than imaginative. Campbell looked round the small hall, with its one olive and three grass green walls, with white cornice and olive green ceiling, and thought rather caustically of a little scenario of Jim and Jean Choosing the Paint. There were a couple of framed Edinburgh prints, very standard wedding present stuff, and the floor covering was sensible hessian.

'Come in here . . . to the kitchen. It's sunny in the afternoons.' Campbell had not thought of Jean as being houseproud, but perhaps she was, of this tidy, practical young-marrieds' kitchen with lots of working surfaces and a place to have breakfast.

'Have a seat.' There was a short vinyl-upholstered bench under the window. Campbell sat down and the dog came over towards him, cocking its head to one side, and sniffed his feet and ankles. 'Shoo her away if she's being a nuisance. . . . Tea? Or coffee?'

'Tea, please.'

'Earl Grey and lemon? Or ordinary Co-op stuff?'

'With lemon, please.'

'Gingerbread?'

'That would be nice.' Campbell sat watching her as she filled a kettle (Russell Hobbs Automatic) and sliced and buttered some home-made-looking gingerbread, wondering if her having-Dr-Campbell-to-tea thing was as simple as it seemed, or was there in it also an element of hostessish self-parody (Earl Grey etc) or was she making a genuine and extravagantly superfluous effort to impress him and was she as aware of the more radical possibilities as he was. He looked round again and noticed a couple more things about the place. There was a strange heap of little pieces of plastic, evidently a model aircraft kit in preparation, on one of the working surfaces in the kitchen, and directly opposite his window seat and across the hall there was a bedroom in which he could see the corner of a low bed covered by a rumpled duvet and, on the floor near it, a pair of discarded tights.

Jean was doing things with plates and mugs and knives, facing him and leaning over the table, with her hair falling down on either side of her face, and her neckline loose enough to show the top half of her breasts.

'It's a bit crumbly.'

'Mmm?'

'The gingerbread. Sorry. I'm not very good at it yet.'

'It looks delicious,' said Campbell, hoping that that didn't sound as if he were sending up the tea business that she was perhaps being entirely serious about. She smiled and handed him a plate with a couple of pieces of buttered gingerbread on it.

'The tea's not quite there yet.' She waited, then poured two mugs and pulled a chair over to join him in the sunny patch by the window. The dog, lying at a point equidistant from both of them with its head slumped out on its front paws, looked up with melting brown eyes at the gingerbread and drooled a viscous puddle on Jean and Jim's polyurethane-finished stripped pine kitchen floor.

'Go away, Sally,' Jean said in a quiet talking-to-humans voice and the dog got up and walked out into the hall. 'She makes me feel so greedy.'

'It's those Oxfam eyes.'

Jean laughed through a mouthful of gingerbread, letting slip a few crumbs, elegantly. Campbell sat with the sun warm on his neck and shoulders, wondering what she was thinking, and trying to think what she thought he was thinking and then, to make it especially difficult, trying to think what he would think of this sort of thing if he were Jim (who was presumably busy with a frog somewhere) and had got to know about it. He could think of nothing at all to say, and there was a long silence. An ice-cream van chimed inanely outside. Jean looked up, briefly at Campbell, then across her kitchen. He noticed, to his surprise, that her hand was shaking. They sat together in silence. Across the hall the dog, which had disappeared for a little while, had reappeared again and now lay across the bedroom door, glowering at Campbell.

Afterwards, alone out in the square, and thinking for some reason of a poem about withered sedge and no birds singing, Campbell pondered on what had happened. They had sat together through two long rather silent cups of tea, and after the silence had spoken almost like strangers, as though Jean had decided that their closeness, though perfectly acceptable in the Institute, should not invade her home, and that inviting him there might even have been a mistake. They had talked nervously about the problems of large dogs in small flats, about Jim's latest model plane, evidently a Beaufighter, and then eventually returned to their customary safe topic, the patients. But it was not even as simple as that, for as they had talked they had looked at each other searchingly, as though they were both thinking of things other than those they were talking about, possibly even of the same things, but things that could not easily be defined or discussed, and were probably best not tackled then and there. They had very carefully avoided touching each other, even casually, as in passing cups of tea, and, from the time it had gone there during the first five minutes of Campbell's visit, the dog had remained steadfastly at its place of duty, watching his every move.

Campbell was puzzled. Had Jean innocently created and then later recognised and retreated from a possibly compromising scene? Or had she decided on something more positive and then changed her mind? Or was she simply reassuring herself, as married women were said to do, that she remained attractive to men other than her husband?

He could guess only dimly at the determinants of her behaviour, and scarcely less dimly at those of his own. Had he, through diffidence, failed to press for something that he wanted very much and that Jean may well have wanted too? Or had he, for the duration of a perfectly straightforward afternoon tea, refrained from meddlesome and probably vain intervention into what might well be a perfectly happy marriage? Or was it conceivable that in Jean there was an element of the bored randy housewife so indispensable to the stag mag hacks and the correspondents in the letter columns of glossy soft porn? That thought barely survived its inception. And what sort of chap had frog research and plastic Beaufighters made of our Jim? Had he proved somehow wanting and was the need for a big dog a symptom of grave matrimonial pathology?

Not that the rationale mattered much. Campbell had to admit to himself that what he had done and, more importantly, what he had not done, had been the product of a state of utter tactical disarray. From the time she had first suggested tea to the rather pathetic coda in which she had followed him halfway down the stairs with his vitamin book, predictably left behind in the kitchen, Campbell had been a helpless victim of his hopes and fears, reacting nervously and ineptly in strange and almost frighteningly sacred surroundings. He didn't like dogs. He didn't even like gingerbread, but he had eaten four bits of it.

As he strolled moodily along towards the flat, Snodgrass a dead weight in his hand, a sports car roared to a halt just ahead of him. It was a sky blue Lotus with a sticker on the back window saying 'Happiness is a tight pussy. Make your cat drunk.' Bones screwed his head out of a tiny window and said, 'How about going for a pint somewhere?'

'It's only quarter past four.'

'Somewhere far away?'

'Okay.'

To avoid a repetition of the untoward events surrounding the previous week's consultant ward round, Campbell made a point of coming in early on Friday morning. He arrived just after ten. There was a specimen bottle on his desk. It contained a few inches of someone's large bowel. A note beside it said 'Hope this helps. Love, Jocasta.' As he was hanging up his jacket Ratho came in, all very breezy and back-from-the-hols.

'I must say it's nice to be back. Not that my study leave didn't go well. I read a terrific amount, mainly general background stuff for the honorary lecturer interview next Monday. And I even got a little painting done.'

'Watercolours?' said Campbell. 'Landscapes?'

'No, no. I meant painting around the house. Of course I've always had an interest in art too. . . . It's a question of time really. . . . Anyway it's nice to be back. How did you get on with my clinics?'

'No problems.'

'Oh, good. Everyone all right then? You know, I worried about them.'

'No problems.'

'And the in-patients? I know Dr Creech wanted to give you a little experience while I was on study leave. Did that go all right too?'

'No problems.'

'Of course the house physician's very good.'

'She seems quite competent.'

'I hope you didn't bully her.'

'I don't think so. You could ask her.'

Ratho laughed his stagey ho-ho-ho laugh and said, 'Oh, David. You're so *serious* about everything. I was *joking*. . . . When can we go round together? Just to hand things over properly. Would after your ward round with Dr Fyvie suit you?'

'Sorry. I've got to go and see an exploration of common bile duct on one of her patients.'

'Oh, well. Perhaps later. Three o'clock?'

'That's the unit clinical meeting.'

'Of course. Perhaps I'll just pop round with Dr Moray.'

'That might be best. I'm sorry, but I really am a bit pushed today.'

'Research going all right?'

'Picking up nicely.'

'I'm so glad. So important to get off to a flying start.'

Over the five days or so of Ratho's absence Campbell had forgotten quite how nauseating he was. He recalled a previous conversation with Bertram, his rival for the honorary lectureship, and wondered if anyone in the unit had any time for this latest and least of the dynasty of Ratho. Even Mrs Alexander, who had formerly idolised him, was, Campbell suspected, beginning to realise that his smooth negligence had caused her much preventable suffering. His unexpected return this morning, bringing the prospect of his attendance at the meeting where Campbell would be presenting her case, was an added bonus.

'Good morning, Dr Moray. . . . Feeling better, Dr Campbell?' Rosamund arrived right on time for her weekly ward round and took charge firmly. 'Let's just stay here for a moment and review things from the case notes. Who have we got?'

'Two patients, Dr Fyvie. Mrs Herron and Theresa Murgatroyd. . . . And an empty bed.'

'An empty bed?'

'Mrs Innes died.'

'Oh. Yes. Her. She'd been there at least five months. Such a problem, these blocked beds. I don't know what the geriatricians think they're playing at, leaving these people silting up facilities in hard-pressed acute medical wards. There was something about her, now. . . . Oh, yes. Dr Dempster was doing an isotope study. Was it all right?'

'There were some technical difficulties.' Campbell remembered vividly Bill's exact words when he had discovered that the porter who was taking the allegedly fasting patient along to his scanning laboratory had been persuaded to go via the hospital shop and let her buy some chocolate biscuits. 'He wanted to repeat it.'

'But she died?'

'Yes.'

'I see. . . . Well, I've discussed one or two ulcer patients for the KM trial with Bill. We should be getting someone in fairly soon. . . .' She picked up some case notes from the duty room desk. 'And Mrs Herron?'

'Just about to go across for surgery.'

'Oh, yes. . . . Exploration of common bile duct.'

'Yes. There was a possibility of a gallstone.'

'I'm not entirely happy about it,' said Rosamund. 'But you know what surgeons are like about operating.' Somehow the question of surgery in the case was no longer either her idea or her responsibility. The juniors noted this transition in an exchange of glances. 'And then there's poor Theresa.' She picked up that patient's case folder, which had doubled in thickness over the previous week. 'How is she?'

'Still fairly ill,' said Campbell, meaning she was dying.

Rosamund sighed. 'These marrow failures. They just strike out of the blue. As you know, half the time we never find out what's causing them. But they're always particularly annoying when one is trying to evaluate an advance in treatment. The problem's much commoner in mongols, of course. Dr Dempster's just dug me out a couple of references on that. It makes one wonder if it was wise of him to include her in the KM trial in the first place. One case like this might quite unnecessarily and misleadingly bias the whole series. A chance event in the wrong patient at the wrong time, resulting in a good drug getting a bad name. I might even have a word with Bill and discuss the whole question of her inclusion in the series. How bad was her ulcer?'

Campbell shuffled uncomfortably. 'It was . . . clinically diagnosed. It wasn't actually proved at barium meal.'

'Oh.' Rosamund pursed her lips. 'I'll speak to Bill. It's rather beginning to sound as if she should never have been in the trial at all. Oh, and one other thing, Dr Campbell: you did ring the priest at St Cuthbert's and keep him informed, didn't you?'

'I . . . saw him. He was in a great hurry.'

'I think now you should probably see him again. See him, not ring him.'

'Yes, Dr Fyvie.'

'Does he know that she co-operated briefly in that series?'

'I think so.'

'Hmmm. Well, you'd better see him and explain the situation as best you can. . . . Stress the random factor.'

A nurse came in and asked for Mrs Herron's case notes, as the porters had come to take her over to Ravelston Orr's theatre.

'So that leaves me with only one patient. . . . One could hardly call that a ward round and justify to oneself one's use of the time. Please carry on, Dr Campbell. I have a drug chap coming shortly and there are some results I want to go over first.'

Campbell and Jean exchanged glances once more. Jean picked up Theresa's case notes and they went into the ward.

A little later in the morning Campbell was sitting in the observation gallery of Ravelston Orr's operating theatre. He was alone, as Jean had been too busy to come over. Only six months previously Campbell had been a house surgeon in the unit and he found his return visit strangely disorienting and kept having to remind himself that he was only visiting, that he was not the houseman there any more, that no one was liable to shout at him and give him a list of fifteen things he should have done already, and, most important of all, that he was no longer the slave of Alester Ravelston Orr's every whim.

The current slave was under glass below, in the operating theatre, standing with the new registrar, a man vaguely known to Campbell, who had replaced his friend Hadden in the post. They were gloved and gowned and waiting. An orderly wheeled the patient in. Mrs Herron looked even more jaundiced under the theatre lights than she had done in the ward. Beside the head of the trolley walked a junior anaesthetist, squeezing a black rubber bag to ventilate the patient. He was upright and neat, even in theatre whites, and his hair was trimmed in the guards-officer style, just this side of decadence. It was Baird-Brown, a coincidence which Campbell vaguely relished, as it added another familiar variable to the evolving scene below.

Ravelston Orr came in, puffing a little, and half turning round to mutter to the little nurse who scuttled along behind him, tying the tabs of his gown. He seemed to have put on weight and his features appeared coarser than Campbell had recalled. He started to wash Mrs Herron's abdomen, using a swab in forceps with vast, billposting gestures, then he draped all but the right upper quadrant of the abdomen, exhibiting even at this early stage a certain acerbity towards his two assistants.

Behind the glass of the observation gallery, Campbell could see everything and hear virtually nothing. Recollections of Ravelston Orr's table manners and appalling tantrums came flooding back, so that the ex-house surgeon felt like a comfortably retired Old Contemptible settling down to watch a silent film of some awful battle which he, at least, had survived, in the full expectation of having some painful memories refreshed.

Gavin Laird, Ravelston Orr's senior registrar, then and still, had come into theatre, in whites but not scrubbed and gowned, and was lurking near the wall behind the chief.

Ravelston Orr's knife was poised. Campbell remembered the results of the various tests for clotting factors in Mrs Herron's blood. All had been just within the safety limits for surgery. Ravelston Orr, who was never happy coping with bleeding problems, might be in for an interesting morning. After his first cut there was a flurry of steel as he and his first assistant clamped a line of bleeds just under the skin. When each bleeding point had been either tied with silk or fried by diathermy, Ravelston Orr made a kind of stiff exaggerated bow to the nurse on his left, a gesture which, as all who had ever worked with him knew, meant no courtesy but simply that he wished his brow to be mopped. It was rather early in the operation for that.

At the head of the operating table Baird-Brown bent over the knobs and bottles of his gassing machine. Campbell wondered if anaesthetist and surgeon had ever talked to one another, and if so what had been said. They did not seem a pair that anyone would have made a point of introducing for anything but the starkest of professional contact. Baird-Brown's account of the operation culminating in Ravelston Orr's knife-throwing trick with the hapless McGavigan came once more to mind.

About twenty minutes after the beginning of the operation, when Ravelston Orr appeared to be making his way under the liver to the common bile duct there was a sudden and dramatic disruption in theatre, which Campbell saw mainly in dumb show, though later, over a pint with the anaesthetist, who survived, verbal details did emerge. A small disturbance, which Campbell, from the distance of the gallery, could not immediately understand, occurred in the operating field. Moments later Ravelston Orr roared like a wounded elephant and, from being crouched over the patient for access to the liver, shot straight into the upright position with his hands up, palms forward and elbows bent, in stiff theatrical surprise. He also dropped his knife.

With the surgeon's head and shoulders out of the way Campbell could see the operating field more clearly, but still could not work out what was wrong, though there did seem to be something odd about the hands around it. Registrar and houseman stood as they had done before their chief's abrupt change of posture. The houseman had both hands on a retractor held against the liver. The registrar had a pair of artery forceps in one hand and a swab in the other. Suddenly Campbell saw what was wrong and what had so upset his old mentor. There was a fifth hand, yellow, like the gloved hands of the assistants, but emerging, unlike them, from *under* the green drapes, and clenched firmly over the left-hand side of the wound, pulling it back to give a remarkably good exposure of the gall bladder and its associated vessels. Mrs

Herron, the ideal patient, was helping with her own operation.

Mr Alester Ravelston Orr unfroze slowly from his statuesque tetany, and moved with fists clenched before him, eyes set in vengeful fury and all his body trembling, from the side of the table up towards Baird-Brown, who was sitting on a stool by his machine still doing a crossword. Surgeon stood for a moment behind anaesthetist, perhaps trying to decide whether to strangle him, knock his head off or merely kick his ribs in. In the end he swung on one foot, and with a huge powerful scything movement of the other, knocked the stool from under Baird-Brown.

Baird-Brown sprawled, his arms flying wide, throwing pencil and *Telegraph* across the theatre in opposite directions, then landed on his back on the floor, and lay crossing himself and muttering, most probably in prayer.

A senior anaesthetist, a rather rustic man whom Campbell knew and liked, who was nominally in charge of anaesthetising Ravelston Orr's lists regardless of which of the juniors actually did them, had come into theatre just in time to witness Ravelston Orr's summary justice on his deputy. He had a mask dangling under his chin, and carried in one hand a cup of coffee and in the other the morning's *Scotsman*, open at the sports page. He looked round then spoke. Campbell heard later that his first words, which broke an awed silence marred only by Baird-Brown's mumbled prayers, were 'Dearie me, I can't turn my back for a minute, but something happens.'

Gavin Laird, the senior registrar, who had been hovering in theatre since the beginning of the operation, was first to move to restore order. He approached the table from the patient's left, and, sliding a hand under the drapes on to Mrs Herron's arm, had removed her hand from the place where its presence had caused so much disturbance. As he did so, Campbell was surprised to see him leaning towards the patient's head, apparently talking to her. He heard later that he had said, 'There, there, Mrs Herron. You'll soon be back to sleep.' If he had said this, it may have been meant as a joke, since it was likely that Mrs Herron's intervention had been reflex rather than conscious.

Ravelston Orr left theatre and did not return. Gavin Laird scrubbed and continued the operation. No gallstone was found, which confirmed the widely held belief that there was no remediable cause for the patient's jaundice, and that she was suffering, as had been thought originally, from the progressive fatal disease known as primary biliary cirrhosis.

On the grass after lunch Campbell told Jean about Mrs Herron's operation: she was half amused, and half horrified, the latter probably as a result of having trained elsewhere and therefore not knowing about Alester Ravelston Orr.

'Are they keeping her?'

'No. They think her liver problem will cause more trouble than the wound. So we're getting her back. She's probably in the ward already.'

'They would have bleeped me. I'll see her as soon as she comes over.'

Campbell was lying on his back, Jean on her side. They were closer together than they would have been if she had got down on the grass first. She was making a daisy chain. Once more Campbell reflected that anyone who had been seeing them in the general mess and on the lawn over the last week or so would have assumed that they had embarked upon, or were about to embark upon the sort of affair not uncommon among junior medical staff. Perhaps they still were: Jean had been acting as if the confusing tea-session had never happened. Campbell closed his eyes and thought of what should have happened instead of the jerky, nervous, dog-ridden, gingerbread-bloated episode, the memory of which was torture still. He felt a light, ticklish touch across his neck.

'What are you doing?'

'Tying you down. With my daisy chain.'

'To take advantage of my helplessness?'

'Only if I feel I'm wanted.'

Campbell made a randy, growling noise and opened his eyes in time to catch Jean's face unawares: she looked soft and vulnerable. On seeing her so, perhaps, did Campbell. Afterwards, when he was thinking about this moment, which he did for most of the afternoon, he wondered if, had they not been on a crowded lawn in the middle of a hospital, it might have lasted a little longer.

'How d'you feel about your case?'

'The presentation? Mrs Alexander?'

'Yes.'

'Oh, not too nervous. I did one or two for that unit meeting thing when I was a houseman.'

'I haven't. Yet.'

'I'm sure Dr Bertram will get round to you.'

'D'you want Mrs Alexander in for the meeting?'

'Sure. Must have the metronidazole miracle on show.'

'I suppose she is a bit better.'

'A bit? She's a minor triumph of modern therapeutics, that's what she is. No temp. No tenderness. The little pills have even taken years off her.'

'You're beginning to sound like them.' Jean had started another daisy chain.

'Bertram? Ratho?'

'And Bill Dempster. All dramas of modern medicine. Thinking and talking mainly about the one case in every ten or so you can do something about.'

'Hmm. I see what you mean.'

'I worry more about the rest.'

'You're a model housegirl.'

'Really, David. Mrs Herron. Look at her. And Theresa.'

After Rosamund's brief appearance they had gone together into the side room where Theresa lay, pale and exhausted. Campbell remembered her sunken eyes and bleeding encrusted gums. A cheap luxuriant glossy auburn-mouse wig had scarcely helped.

'We're still trying with Theresa,' said Campbell. 'Sometimes the marrow just picks up and does everything properly again. We don't know it's not going to, so we've got to try.'

'I put up the drips,' said Jean. 'She does her best to keep still and all that, but it does hurt her.' She paused in lovely contemplation. 'D'you really think it's worth it? All the platelets and blood and so on.'

'Modern medicine's got to try and pull her out of it,' said Campbell, 'because modern medicine dropped her in it.'

'That KM stuff?'

'Most probably. I heard Bill say they're checking up on the

blood of everyone who's on it.'

'In summary then, an interesting and instructive case which serves to remind us of one or two useful points about the differential diagnosis of chronic diarrhoea. The history, as almost always in gastro-intestinal disease, offers much, especially when it is remembered that in these days in which world-wide travel has developed to a stage where it is both commonplace and rapid, tropical diseases have consequently become tropical only in their origins.' That sentence had caused Campbell particular trouble during the preparation of his case, but he felt the effort worthwhile: it had the pompous resounding obscurity of proper medical English. Its effect on the audience was gratifying: the senior students had looked puzzled and the front bench, consisting of all four consultants from Creech's unit plus three from a sister unit with which reciprocal clinical-meeting attendance was customary, nodded sagely.

'The case also illustrates the value of simple side-room methods in diagnosis.' Creech smiled to himself, perhaps thinking comfortable thoughts about the optional extra on his microscope. 'And, if one can say so without claiming undue diagnostic zeal and expertise, the case also shows the value of an open-minded approach to diagnosis in follow-up clinics.' That was the nearest Campbell allowed himself to come in his formal presentation to calling Ratho a fool. He wondered if it was near enough. Probably yes: Ratho was looking distinctly uncomfortable, shifting in his seat and glancing round to see if people were looking at him. There was no especial reason why they should be, as Campbell had punctiliously refrained from naming the clinician whose negligence he had so delicately unveiled. Bertram, by contrast, was looking very pleased with himself. He lounged back puffing three-foot smoke rings from his pipe. Campbell remembered their rivalry for the honorary lectureship.

'Now Mrs Alexander has kindly agreed to come along and answer any questions you might have.' Campbell went to the door and signalled to a staff nurse who was waiting outside with the patient. Both came in and Mrs Alexander sat down in a chair reserved for her, facing the audience. The staff nurse stood at her side.

Creech leaned forward and coughed. 'How do you feel now, Mrs Alexander?'

'Wonderful, thank you, Dr Creech.' Campbell noted that farther back in the audience Ratho was blushing deeply.

'How did you feel this time last week?'

'Terrible. Really terrible.'

Creech half turned towards the audience. 'They do, you know. They feel terrible. I had it myself, of course. Before metronidazole.'

One of the senior students asked what the previous biopsies had shown. Campbell said that if anyone had any more questions for Mrs Alexander they should ask them now, and technicalities could be discussed later. Ratho squirmed.

'Well, if there are no more questions for Mrs Alexander, we'll let her go,' said Campbell. 'Thank you very much for coming along, Mrs Alexander.'

'On the contrary, thank you, Dr Campbell. Thank you very much for everything you've done.' Her typical hyperbole was matched with a cloyingly grateful smile. She got up and strode out with her escort, casting, as she did so, a very cold look at Ratho. Bertram was gazing peacefully out of the window.

When she had gone the senior student repeated his question about the thoroughness of the previous investigations. Campbell looked appropriately thoughtful and said, 'There may have been a previous biopsy. Or of course the report may have gone missing.' Creech, who had displayed a little anxiety when the question was repeated, was clearly relieved by the way Campbell had handled it. No one in medicine gains from the too public discussion of negligence.

In his capacity as chairman Creech thanked Campbell for his presentation and the business of the meeting moved on to another of Bill Dempster's interesting cases. On the whole, Campbell thought his case had not gone too badly. No one in the audience had fallen asleep and Jean, who had been watching him intently throughout, might conceivably have been impressed. Only one of his slides had been projected upside down and his two references to the pioneering wartime work of the senior consultant had gone down well in the front row. Campbell sat happily through the rest of the meeting and when it was over walked upstairs to the Sister's room on the female ward with Bertram. He was complimentary, and in his new role of coach, and junior patron of Campbell's medical fortunes, reminded him of what he had said previously about the benefits to be gained from a short period looking after Creech's female in-patients. 'The chief did say this morning that he'd been quite pleased. Of course you've got a very good house physician here.'

'Yes. She seems okay.'

'Mind you, I get the impression he's going off Ratho. This interview on Monday might be difficult for poor Fraser.'

'Really?'

'And in a way it's a pity from Fraser's point of view that that case of yours came up today.'

Campbell recalled that Bertram had been instrumental in its selection. They had tea and ate most of the sandwiches. Suddenly the door burst open and Fraser Ratho came in, white and shaking. He ignored Bertram and rounded on Campbell. 'David Campbell . . . I think you're . . . a j-jolly rotter.'

Campbell put down his cup and stood up. He decided that the best thing to do would be to play very dumb and let him get on with it and get it all out of his system. Perhaps it was just as well that Bertram was there as a witness. 'Sorry,' he said. 'You'd better explain.'

'P . . , p . . . presenting that case. . . . Just like that. . . . Without so much as even discussing it with me. . . . And especially Mrs Alexander.' He was red and beginning to splutter.

'She didn't mind. I asked her. She agreed.'

'That's not what I mean. . . . As well you know.'

'Sorry,' said Campbell. 'I don't.'

Ratho was still ignoring Bertram, who was lighting his pipe with ostentatious preoccupation, wielding a Wilsonian flame-throwing lighter that roared and crackled. He sucked and puffed and smacked his lips and blew a billowing cloud of bluish-grey smoke. Ratho's jaw went loose and for a moment Campbell wondered if he was going to cry. 'I suppose you're well aware that just about half Monday's committee just happened to be sitting in the front row.'

'No,' said Campbell, which was almost true. He had latterly suspected it, from the smug expression on Bertram's face during the meeting. With a little more nursing Bertram's pipe had settled down to a healthy glow. He looked up as if he had just noticed Ratho. 'Oh. Hello, Fraser. Have some tea.'

'No thank you, Dr Bertram. . . . David Campbell, I still think you're a . . . jolly rotter.'

When he had gone Bertram sucked at his pipe. 'I don't think I'd feel so sorry for the poor bugger if he could even swear properly.' He got up and remarked, 'A nice case, David. A nice case,' then walked out, smiling to himself.

'Dr Campbell? There's a Mr Herron here wants a word with you. . . . He's quite upset.' A red-haired third-year student nurse was looking at him from the doorway of Sister's room. Campbell felt guilty at having sat alone so long over tea.

'The cirrhosis lady's husband?'

'Yes. Him.'

'I'll see him now if he wants.'

'I don't know if he wanted to see you in particular. He said anyone in charge.'

'Well, I'm sort of in charge of Rosamund's beds. I don't mind seeing him.'

'Dr Campbell. . . .'

'What, nurse?'

'Did you know she's just died?'

Campbell was completely taken aback by the sudden death of someone he had expected to die slowly. 'What? When did that happen? What happened?'

'She collapsed. About twenty minutes ago.'

Campbell was also surprised that Jean had not told him. 'Who certified her? Dr Moray?'

'Yes. She's with the daughters now. But Mr Herron wants to see someone in charge.'

'Okay. I suppose it would be all right to see him in here. . . .'

'The daughters are in the visitors' room.'

'Thanks, nurse. Just send him in.'

Campbell stood up and put his empty cup with the others on the tray. The nurse showed Mr Herron in. Though he had been meaning to have a word with his dying patient's husband ever since he had taken over her care, Campbell had not so much as glimpsed him prior to this meeting. He was about five foot ten and precisely dressed, as a middle-aged man might be for a good office job. He wore the blue and white boys' tie of a school about three-quarters way down the Edinburgh snobbery league. His eyes, behind gold-rimmed glasses, looked more angry than sad, and his hands were shaking. Campbell remembered that this was the man who, according to Jean, had been planning a holiday for when his wife got out of hospital.

'Dr Campbell?'

'Mr Herron?'

'Yes. . . . Julia Herron's . . . Julia Herron . . . was my wife.'

Campbell asked him to sit down. He did so, leaning forward with a hand clenched on each knee. There was an awkward silence, as though neither knew where to begin, or indeed what had to be discussed.

Campbell leaned towards Mr Herron's chair and said, 'I was very sorry to hear that your wife . . .' then found that he couldn't finish the sentence. He looked away from Mr Herron and when he looked back saw that he was crying, with his face cupped in his hands and his shoulders jerking. The student nurse came with two cups of tea, put them down and left again in pitying silence. Mr Herron took his hands away from his face, glanced with surprise at the tea then put his hands up to his face again and sobbed more loudly than before. Campbell reflected, not for the first time, on how the Institute answered the immediate needs of the bereaved: a cup of tea, a bundle of clothes and certificate from a big blue book making it all tidy and legal.

Why had she died so soon? He had expected her to linger for a few more weeks, yellow and puffy with her fluid and electrolyte problems getting more and more difficult and then impossible, at which point someone, probably Rosamund, would decide that modern medicine had done its best and further treatment, being impracticable, should not be attempted. Campbell was puzzled and discomfited to be talking to a relative in these circumstances and wished that he had heard more, preferably from Jean, about what had happened. As

Mr Herron sobbed, Campbell noticed to his further surprise that there were traces of blood, still moist, around the fingernails of the new widower's right hand.

That was odd. As he began his fourth cup of tea of the afternoon an unpleasant thought struck Campbell. When Mr Herron's sobbing subsided he enquired, as gently as possible, 'Were you with her . . . when . . . ?'

Mr Herron looked up. 'Yes . . . with the girls. . . .'

'Oh. Was it . . . very upsetting for them . . . ?'

He sobbed again. 'It was horrible . . . really horrible. The wee girl got covered.'

'Covered ?'

'Yes. When she was sick. Covered in blood.'

'Oh God,' said Campbell involuntarily. 'Where is she now ?'

'With the junior doctor . . . Dr . . .'

'Moray.'

'Yes. With her. And the nurses. They've sort of cleaned her up.' He sat up and stared at Campbell. Her sudden demise was explained. She had died of a massive internal haemorrhage, a predictable and not uncommon end for cirrhotics. Mr Herron looked blankly at Campbell and said, 'But I'm still going to sue.'

'Sue ?' said Campbell. 'What for ?'

'Everything,' said Mr Herron in a flat voice. 'Even the girl's clothes, I suppose, though that's the least of it. . . . No, the things that'll really drag this place's name through the mud'll be the bigger things.'

'Bigger things ?'

'The operation.'

'Operation ?'

'The operation that killed her. This time last week she was getting better. The terrible itching was going away and we'd made plans to go off on holiday when she got out and then three hours after your marvellous operation she's dead. It'll all come out in the enquiry.'

Campbell put down his tea and listened.

'There's bound to be an enquiry. People don't just die in three hours after an operation that's so straightforward that even patients' husbands don't get told about it.'

'I don't think anyone underestimated the seriousness of the

operation. It would have been explained to her when she signed the permission slip.' (It *should* have been explained.)

'That's not the point.'

Legally, it *was* the point.

'And there's the whole business of experimentation without consent. One day earlier this week I had a most interesting chat just outside the ward with a priest – I'm not a Catholic myself of course, though I have many Catholic acquaintances – but this priest, a most interesting and highly intelligent man, alerted me to various possibilities that might be contributing to my wife's decline. That too, would come out at a proper enquiry. He mentioned some tablets that people seemed to be getting whether they needed them or not. And an unfortunate case within his professional knowledge. I didn't pay much attention at the time, but by chance the subject came up in the staff room at work – I teach at a fairly important school here in town – (he was fingering his tie) and quite a few of my colleagues' views gave cause for anxiety.' He paused. 'Can you personally guarantee that no irregularities have occurred?'

Campbell opened his mouth to speak but Mr Herron interrupted him. 'You don't have to say anything meantime. It'll all come out at the enquiry.'

'I was going to say that it's distressing for everybody when someone dies. I only heard about it a few minutes ago myself, and I'm sort of shocked too, in a different, lesser way to you, but still shocked. We thought she was doing quite well, but we knew she had a serious illness.'

'*You* knew.'

'Didn't you? Dr Moray said she'd spoken to you.'

Mr Herron sniffed and put his hands round the cup in front of him. 'I thought if it had been serious I would have seen someone in charge. I'd a holiday booked, you know,' he said in the same flat voice. 'I suppose I could sue about that too. Not being told.'

'I'm sorry you feel that way about it,' said Campbell. The man sitting in front of him, with his hands clasped sacramentally round their solid institutional teacup, was both tragic and pathetic. He sniffed and blinked and tossed his head back a little.

'I'm not without influence, you know. A head of department, with connections in the legal world. And my wife was an active canvasser for our MP.' He fingered his tie again, perhaps to convey he was a Mason too. 'I've never had cause for complaint against the medical profession before.' He stood up and Campbell stood up too. Mr Herron spoke again. 'But seeing my wife vomiting blood one moment and lying there dead the next . . . perhaps unnecessarily . . . has given me . . . new insight . . . and indeed resolution.'

He probably taught English, Campbell decided, as the man squared up to leave. Once more he noticed the fingers of his right hand.

'Would you like something to wash your hands?'

The man said nothing, but looked back at Campbell, his face a tense, changing map of tightly held emotions, including perhaps pity and a strange hurt irony.

Campbell went along to Rosamund's room and negotiated his way past the secretary to tell his consultant what had happened. She stopped writing as he talked, but did not put her pen down.

'I don't think there will be any problems.'

'No?'

'Dr Moray rang me right away. I rang the Procurator Fiscal to keep the law informed. Just by way of courtesy really. He was most sympathetic, as well he might have been, there being nothing amiss. However, it is best to keep the law informed, and sooner rather than later.'

'There were some problems though.'

'Really?'

'At the operation this morning.'

'What sort of problems?'

Feeling that no very good cause was being served by his frankness, Campbell outlined the small anaesthetic mishap.

'Not contributory,' said Rosamund after a moment's silence. 'In the unlikely and unfortunate event of that episode becoming public knowledge it would be deemed both non-contributory and nothing to do with us.' Rosamund looked down once more to what she was writing.

'The husband seemed very upset,' said Campbell.

'But he knows nothing of the incident you described.'

'No.'

'Even if he did, no solicitor would touch it,' said Rosamund. 'Sad he's upset though. Perhaps if you spent more time talking to relatives at all stages of the patient's illness . . . and less watching surgical operations, Dr Campbell. . . . However, in this case I think everything will be all right. I take it there was never any question of her co-operating in the evaluation of KM 1103.'

'No, Dr Fyvie.'

'Thank you for coming along, Dr Campbell.'

Jean was waiting outside Rosamund's door. She was pale and clearly agitated.

'Oh, David, it was so awful. . . .' She was standing close, facing him. 'It just happened . . . horribly, really horribly.' Her lips were trembling and she was not far from tears.

'It sounded horrible.' They turned and began to walk back to the ward.

'It was. I got there just before she died. I've never seen anything like it. Blood everywhere. And the kids . . . it was just awful. There wasn't anything I could do. I speeded up her drip, full open, and tried to get some blood from the fridge, but she was going even before we got it. I tried as hard as I could.'

'It doesn't sound as if there was much chance.'

'I wondered about that, and the awful thing was that it made me feel that maybe I shouldn't have been trying at all. I felt in the way. I didn't know what to do about the family, and Mr Herron was shooing them away but didn't want to go away himself and it just got so confused, then the duty gasman came and looked and just said, "She's a goner." I think he thought Mr Herron was a doctor here. I nearly cried, really.' She was nearly crying again. 'Oh, David, it was awful.'

'Sounds hellish.'

'Oh, it was, it was. And I felt so useless.'

'I'm sure you coped as well as anyone could have.'

'I wish you'd been there.'

'I wouldn't have made any difference. She must have bled

from varices. Bled gallons. And not clotted. Nothing could have helped.'

'I still felt useless.'

'I'm sure you were fine. And Mr Herron told me you coped with the kids too.'

'The nurses did mainly. I just helped with one.'

'Was that awful too?'

'Fairly. The one kid I had just clung to me and cried, "Mummy, mummy," and wouldn't let go. That made me feel useless too, and a bit to blame.'

'You're not.'

'I felt it though.'

They had walked back as far as Sister's room. An auxiliary saw them and said, 'I put some fresh tea in for you, doctors.' Wanly, Jean thanked her, and they sat down in the little room once more, and talked for a long time about death and medicine and Mrs Herron. Jean did most of the talking. Campbell listened. Everything she said made him think more highly of her. Even her inexperience, her shockability, was appealing, and through it came the compassionate intelligence that had characterised everything he knew of her clinical work. Only a few months qualified, she had been caught defenceless, hopelessly involved in the death of a patient. She would learn.

Eventually they talked of other things, and of other patients. They got round once more to Theresa.

'David, I meant to tell you. The priest chap rang in. He'd like to come in and see somebody.'

'I'll see him. Tomorrow. Nine o'clock. No. Half past.'

'Okay. I'll tell him. Saturday? Will you be in?'

'I suppose so. Most people come in, if only to look keen or impress Creech or get away from their wives or whatever. And when in Rome. . . . How's Theresa?'

'Pretty flat. Her pressure's down and she looks a bit toxic.'

'I hope tomorrow'll be soon enough.'

'Oh, I think it will be. Unless something else happens.'

'You on tonight?'

'No, I'm not. We split the weekends now. Whoever does Friday gets Saturday and Sunday off and the other way round. Dr Hamilton's on tonight. That was the other other thing.'

'What was?'

'Are you going to this unit beer and skittle thing?'

'Oh that. Tonight? I'd sort of forgotten about it . . . with all this. Paid my money though. So I suppose I'll go.'

'I thought I might as well go too. Will you give me a lift?'

'Sure. Your car off the road?'

'No. Jim's taking it. He's going off for the weekend.'

'Is he?' said Campbell, trying to make it sound casual.

'Sailing. He quite often does if I'm on most of the weekend.'

'What time do you want picked up?'

'Say half past seven. Residency steps?'

'Half past seven.'

After that Campbell did not really concentrate very well on his vitamin review. He sat looking out of the window, thinking sometimes about Mrs Herron and sometimes about Jean and the various possibilities opening out from their short conversation, until it was time to go across to the pub at five. There he met Hadden again, but deliberately did not drink much. He left in good time to walk over to the flat to pick up his car, then drove back to the Institute and his rendezvous with Jean.

She came out of the Residency looking marvellous, but unexpectedly marvellous, in faded old jeans, scruffy but very clean, and a loose pullover. She climbed into his car and sat beside him, smelling of just having had a bath, and of a new perfume, not her usual one, which, like her voice and the colour of her eyes, was permanently imprinted on Campbell's consciousness.

'Will you look after my purse, David? There isn't room in these jeans for me and things in the pockets as well.'

'Okay.'

She put on a safety belt, which had the effect of rediscovering her breasts, hitherto lost in her pullover, and making Campbell feel so randy that he wondered if his road sense might be affected. They drove towards the suburban pub where the beer and skittles evening was to be held. Campbell did not know the way but Jean did. He wondered about suggesting a drink at an intermediate pub and then gently diverting the expedition from its stated goal, perhaps instead to another drink somewhere and a walk along the beach at dusk or something like that. Glancing at her profile, and discerning in it a sense of purpose even in the pursuit of leisure, Campbell decided not even to suggest it. A lift there might reasonably be held to imply a lift back, which left possibilities for later.

They got to the pub a little later than most people. It was very much a unit affair, organised by the downstairs staff nurses, who had taken names and money a full week before, which was why Campbell had forgotten about it. He recognised with distaste a number of people he had not expected to attend, such as the Sister from the male ward, who was wearing absurdly tight tan slacks and giggling a great deal to conceal her true age. Campbell had the feeling that when she had drunk a little more still she might go quieter, if not curl up in a corner and go to sleep, as she was said to have done on a previous similar occasion. Bertram had not arrived. Bill Dempster was organising people, with the help of a stranger, a little man in a loud check sports jacket with a lapel badge saying, 'Mike Forrest: Area Sales Manager: K & M.' That was an unexpected and unpleasant aspect of the beer and skittles evening.

Bill introduced them before avoiding action could be taken. He had a music-hall Lancashire accent and unstoppable salesmanlike bonhomie. 'Pleased to meet you, Dr Moray. Dr Campbell, very pleased to meet you.' First he kissed Jean's hand, with a dapper little bow, then gave Campbell a firm, possibly Masonic handshake. 'Now how about something to drink . . .? Compliments of K & M of course. Expense no object . . . Gin and tonic, Dr Moray? . . . Or a wee Jock and Doris, as you hielanders say. Beer for you, Dr Campbell? Your own very fine local brew is in excellent condition in this hostelry, is it not, Dr Dempster?'

Jean took her usual half pint of cider. Campbell took the same. Bill wrote their names up on a blackboard, putting them in different teams. 'Rule of the house. I thought of it myself. If you come together you play in different teams. Mixes everybody up. Right, David?'

A few more people arrived, including Dr Kyle, the second senior consultant, who, in a blazer and check shirt with a silk cravat, looked a little too well dressed either to enjoy himself or play skittles very well, but none the less proceeded to do both. Ratho arrived with his wife and Campbell remembered the circumstances in which their troth, according to Bertram's version, had been plighted. She was indeed bigger than he was, and if anything more unprepossessing. Over the evening Campbell got the feeling that they were consciously avoiding him. Bertram and his wife, a buoyant blonde ex-staff nurse from the unit (their romance was houseman and night-nurse, a hospital classic), rolled in holding each other up and singing, pretending to be much more drunk than they were, which was fairly.

In addition to the people Campbell knew, there was an incomprehensible social fringe, a chorus of peasants and townspeople, possibly hangers-on of unit hangers-on. One of them, a barrel-shaped little man wearing a green blazer with a Cameronians badge, introduced himself as the husband of the part-time glassware washer from Dr Creech's laboratory. He explained to Campbell that he was in the medical line himself, being a traveller in barbers' sundries.

Campbell drank very little, because he had the feeling that he had last experienced on Wednesday afternoon, that he was liable to find himself going operational at short notice, and wanted very much to put up a better tactical showing than he had done on that occasion. He played skittles in his turn, and watched Jean as she played. When she bowled she did so as if nothing else mattered, least of all dignity. She hurled herself forward with a kind of concentrated abandon, scoring high, mainly strikes. Watching her for the first time in violent physical action, Campbell considerably expanded his ideas on what she might be like in bed. His previous estimate, postulating a sort of contained grace, underwent drastic revision. Between their turns to bowl they drifted together and talked.

Someone announced an interval for sausage rolls and yet more drinks. The K & M salesman dotted round, more than ever a music-hall turn, dispensing wisecracks and largesse. Campbell overheard him telling Mrs Ratho, fully two feet taller, that he hoped there were no surgeons present, because K & M had some marvellous stuff for ulcers that was going to put half of them out of a job. At the end of the interval Bill, loud, confident and a bit drunk proposed a vote of thanks to the drug company and made a stupid remark about anyone whose ulcer had been tickled up by the evening's festivities being able to get just the thing from Mr Forrest on the way out after the remainder of the contest.

Jean did not seem very amused and looked at her watch and then at Campbell. He said something vague about getting enough of a good thing and somehow it was arranged that they were leaving there and then. Campbell found Bill to tell him to rub out their names from the teams.

'David. . . . I was looking for you. Just a quick word.'

'Oh?'

'Yes. . . . I wonder if you could do me a real favour.'

'What?'

'ICU.'

'When?'

Bill smiled his decent-guy smile and said, 'I'm sorry the notice is kind of short. Tomorrow actually. Can you do it?'

Campbell was about to tell him, in more or less diplomatic terms, to fuck off, when he remembered that Jean was on duty for Creech's unit on Saturday and therefore would be spending the night in the Institute. With expressions of mild inconvenience and a modest show of reluctance, he agreed.

'Great, David. I'll take one of your nights. Just say the word. Any time. Well, almost any time. We'll discuss it nearer the time. Thanks a helluva lot. I don't know what I'd have done if you couldn't have managed.'

'Don't mention it.'

'Thanks, David.'

'David . . .?'

'What?'

'I want to go back to the Institute.'

'Theresa?'

'Yes.'

'Let's. I was wondering about her.'

'Haemoglobin?'

'No. More the clotting things. And infection.'

'I thought of that. Did some blood cultures.'

'I was going to ask you.'

'I did them anyway.'

'Anything back?'

'Nothing.'

They drove down the hill towards the centre of town, through blue summer dusk. After the skittle alley the car was quiet. They did not talk much. In front of them Edinburgh's profile was etched on the darkening blue: the three spires of a cathedral in the New Town, the military lump of the castle, an older cathedral with a crown steeple high on the Royal Mile, and, with its massive clock tower, the Institute itself, squatting, a dead weight of Victorian charity on the north edge of the park.

As he drove Campbell wondered about Jean's apparent lack of concern for the public observation of propriety. In a gossipy unit such as theirs, it must already have been assumed back at the skittle alley that a lot was going on between them. In public they consistently acted as if they were having an affair, and yet in private their behaviour had hitherto been utterly proper. Was she so innocent that it had not occurred to her what people might think; or was she indifferent to it; or was she being a little cleverer than he had thought, and relying perhaps correctly on the reasonable assumption that anyone so obviously not hiding anything had nothing to hide, with a view to taking it from there under that somewhat complex but perhaps effective cover? It was interesting, but not the sort of thing he could very well ask her about at that stage of their relationship.

Campbell parked in the Residency car park and they went straight up to the ward. Just before they reached it they were met by two porters pushing the zinc mortuary trolley, disguised as usual with pillows, sheets and a cheerful pink blanket.

'Theresa Murgatroyd?' Campbell enquired.

'Something like that,' said the rearguard porter.

In the duty room Theresa's case folder lay open, with her last ever progress note, by Dr Hamilton the duty houseman, ready to view. It read, 'Patient collapsed at 2035 following acute GI bleed with vomiting and diarrhoea. Resuscitation attempted without success. Seen again at 2045. No pulse. No respiration. Fixed dilated pupils. Certified dead at 2048. Certificate completed.'

While Campbell read the notes Jean had picked up the blue death certificate book.

'What has she put her down as?'

Jean sniffed. 'Exsanguination. Secondary to gastro-intestinal erosions. Secondary to marrow failure of unknown cause.'

'No mention of drugs?'

'No. Look.'

Campbell took the book, from which the completed certificate had not yet been torn. There was a moist clear drop, with a smudge running from it, blurring the section of the form devoted to the deceased's normal place of residence. In just over a year's qualified experience in his profession, Campbell had not previously seen a tear on a death certificate.

Jean sniffed again. 'Should we try to get permission for a post mortem?'

Campbell remembered the priest whom he was due to see in the morning. 'Catholics as a rule aren't frightfully keen. And that priest has been a bit awkward.'

'You could try. It might help.'

'It wouldn't really. Not about the drug. Once the marrow's knocked off it's knocked off, and you can't say from a PM what's been knocking it off.'

'Should we ring Rosamund?'

'She doesn't much like being rung at home.'

'Or Bill?'

'He'll still be at the beer and skittles.'

'Of course.'

'And he never was very easy to convince that his wonderful KM ulcer cure ever had anything to do with making anyone ill. I phoned him once before about that. He said it could have been aspirin.'

'So that's it.'

'There's nothing else to be done. . . . Except see the priest bloke in the morning.'

'I rang him for you. He said he'd be up about half past nine.'

Jean and Campbell left the ward and walked out past the stairs and on to a raised footway which joined the medical and the surgical corridors of the hospital. It was darker now, but still clear blue. An almost full moon lit the trees and the ghostly empty deck chairs of the Institute's only lawn. There was nothing to say till they got back to the Residency car park.

'Shall I drive you home?'

'Yes please, David.'

They drove round the park and up into Marchmont, where they both lived. He stopped outside her flat. She did not get out immediately. He switched off his engine. She did not invite him up. Instead they sat for a very long time in the car, talking. The moon's pale disc rose among the branches of the trees in the square. Every twenty minutes or so a policeman passed. The first few times he did so, Campbell was aware of him glancing into the car to ensure that nothing was happening in the limited privacy of his decrepit Mini which might imperil the decorum of Marchmont by night. In the dark Jean and Campbell talked and talked. The policeman continued to pass on his round and no longer bothered to look inside. Campbell thought about that, and decided that if the weight of professional opinion (so to speak) was against him, there was little point in trying. Later, as he drove alone the few hundred yards to his own flat shortly after two he reflected that practically the only time they had touched each other had been in the presence of no less a chaperon than Dr H. J. S. Creech, MD, FRCPE, their senior consultant.

At nine fifteen on Saturday morning there was another specimen of colon sitting on Campbell's desk, with a plaintive note from Jocasta which included something about looking forward to hearing from him again soon. He put both to one side, reflecting that it was a pity his lab technician was still, for family reasons, absent. Then he went up to the ward to look round Rosamund's patients. Most of them seemed to have died. Jean was not in the ward. He met her in the duty room: she looked tired and when he spoke to her sounded distant, as though they had talked too long the night before. Campbell wondered if they had chalked up another regrettable occasion, though he had not thought so at the time. They had talked about a whole lot of things in an endlessly proliferating ground-clearing conversation, the sort of thing that people had to have only once or twice while getting to know each other, a kind of extended amalgam of the various shorter sessions on the lawn and in the duty room where they were now. After it Campbell had felt that though physically they were as chaste as ever, they could not remain so for long. She had talked with a quite surprising objectivity about her marriage, and had said various odd things hinting that sex was not what it had been. She had not run her husband down, but had described him with a knowing, qualified realism, in which there was no hint of anything so crude as my-husband-doesn't-understand-me. Nonetheless Campbell had got a distinct impression that after two years or so (they had married as students) they had diverged a little, and a lot of the shine had come off, before the truly binding commitments of career and kids had fixed them for life. He had observed marriages before, from various vantage points, though rarely with as much concern as in this case, and knew a little of the commoner patterns of early pathology. In summary, there were quite a few interesting question marks around Jean and Jim.

Jean and Campbell were discussing the relative merits of their consultants when the priest tapped on the glass of the duty room door. Campbell got up and took him into the little visitors' room off the ward corridor, where bad news was traditionally handed out to relatives. The priest sat down, remarking that he hadn't been too well himself, with his gastric stomach. He then enquired about Theresa.

'I'm afraid she took a turn for the worse last night. . . .'

'I'm sorry to hear that. Very sorry indeed.'

'In fact she bled quite a lot. . . .'

'Oh dear.'

'. . . and because she . . . couldn't clot her blood . . .'

'What's that? What's that?'

'. . . she just . . . carried on bleeding.'

'Is she all right now?'

'No,' said Campbell. 'In fact at about twenty to nine last night. . . .'

'God rest her soul,' said the priest. 'Gathered in and her only fifteen. . . . What was the cause?'

'I tried to talk to you about her illness the other day,' said Campbell. 'You were in a hurry.'

'God's work,' snapped the priest.

'She'd been having trouble with her bone marrow. Not making the various things needed to fight infection and help clot the blood. Not even making very much blood.'

'Was that after her hair fell out?'

'Yes. We tried, with various things, to . . . keep her going. But. . . .'

'Was that anything to do with these fancy tests?' asked the priest.

'No,' said Campbell. 'They're very safe.' He realised immediately how careless a remark that was. The room filled up with the smell of the priest's feet.

'So it was those pills.'

'What pills?' said Campbell, trying to find out how much the priest knew about the KM trial.

'Those KM 1103 things. For ulcers.'

'It's almost impossible to say. . . . People's marrows can stop for almost no reason.'

'I must say I don't like the sound of that.'

'She didn't have many,' said Campbell, once more a bit off guard.

'Many what?'

'Oh. Of those pills.'

'I'm not so sure I like the sound of this at all,' said the priest.

'We did our best,' said Campbell. 'Dr Fyvie took a personal interest in her case.'

'Buying her a wig indeed. When you were killing her with experiments.'

'Father Herdman. I don't think you can really say that,' said Campbell, who couldn't see why he shouldn't. There was an awkward silence which ended abruptly when the door of the visitors' room opened and Dr Rosamund Fyvie came in.

'Father Herdman! Dr Moray said you'd be here. Thank you, Dr Campbell.' She took Campbell's seat; he stood by, hoping that she would have a tougher time than she had had in her previous encounter with the priest, who was now sitting so far forward that Campbell, bearing Herdman's halitosis in mind, felt a little sorry for Rosamund.

The priest stared into her eyes and said, 'Dr Campbell here and I have just been going into this whole question of using an innocent fifteen-year-old mongol child for the purposes of a guinea pig and human experimentation.'

'Father Herdman,' Rosamund sighed patiently. 'Of course you're upset by Theresa's death. We all are.' She paused for a moment of being upset. 'But to be so overcome by it as to misunderstand our efforts here so . . . completely . . . seems hardly in keeping with the . . . dignity of your office.'

'It was those tablets,' said the priest.

Rosamund gazed at him with an expression of infinite patience and understanding. 'Up and down the country hundreds of patients have taken thousands and thousands of doses of the drug you and I are discussing, and nothing but benefit has accrued.'

'Little Theresa's dead.'

'For reasons, in all probability, not remotely connected with those tablets. Of which she had, in any case, only six or seven.'

'Is that a fact?'

'Many individual patients have now taken hundreds without ill effect. It's one of the most promising drugs I've ever been called upon to evaluate. And, I think, one of the safest too.'

'Is that a fact?'

'The only side effect reported so far has been an increase in appetite. And that mainly in the people who've had the very worst ulcers. I really don't think the safety of the drug can be questioned. Even before it reached the stage of clinical evaluation it had to pass the most stringent of government safety tests. . . . It came through. With flying colours.'

'Oh well,' said the priest.

'However,' Rosamund went on. 'If ever the question of its safety were to be raised, full records are available for everyone who's ever had the drug so far.'

'Including Theresa?'

'Including Theresa. And if the slightest suspicion of any

undesirable side effect were to arise, her case might still turn out to be of the utmost importance. Even though she had only five or six tablets.'

'Six or seven.'

'The exact figure will be in her case notes, Father Herdman. I can't recall it offhand. As I was saying, Theresa's case might still, in that unhappy event, turn out to be quite crucial.'

'That's not much help to her.'

'True. But it might turn out to be of the greatest significance to others.'

'I suppose so.'

'So there's just a chance that her death may turn out not to be a meaningless tragedy.' Campbell sensed in that an attempt to blame God rather than KM 1103, perhaps a hint too subtle for the priest. 'And if that happens – and we pray it may never – she will not have died in vain.'

Amen, thought Campbell to himself.

'Maybe,' said the priest.

'She may yet turn out to have laid down her life for others,' said Rosamund. Campbell thought that crude, but Rosamund appeared to know her market.

'Hmmph,' said the priest. 'Maybe.'

'There is no greater love than this, Father Herdman. . . . Dr Campbell, I've checked the certificates and so on. Would you kindly fetch them. Father Herdman must be about God's business.'

Campbell went into the duty room to collect the death certificate. Jean was sitting at her desk. She looked up, glad to see him. He explained what he had come for, and she handed him a buff envelope.

'That's it. All neat and tidy.' Their fingers touched under the envelope. Campbell remembered the tear stain on the certificate from the previous night. They looked at each other. More than ever before Campbell felt that she was willing him close to her. He stood with the envelope in his hand, unsure what to do, then made his most positive proposition in the course of their relationship so far.

'Jean, you're on tonight, aren't you?'

'Yes.'

'I'm on duty for the ICU.'

'Are you? Again.'

'Yes. Bill Dempster swopped duties. At least I think it was a swop. So I'll be stuck down there from six.'

'Poor old you.'

'If it's quiet here . . . come down and see me, if you like.'

'Thanks. I will. That'll be nice.'·

By ten that evening Jean had not come down to the ICU to visit Campbell. He had been sitting for four hours, bored and distracted, with nothing to do except think about her, with occasional intervals of trying not to think about her. The unit was full but quiet. He had checked over the patients with a more than ordinarily sullen late duty nurse, and had not yet heard from the night staff, who had been on duty for an hour. It was said that a night in ICU could be totally uneventful: Campbell thought about that for a few moments and succeeded in not thinking about Jean. A quiet night was possible but improbable.

He had brought Snodgrass and a short textbook on liver disease but had not looked at either. He had refrained so far from opening the drawer marked 'Scottish and Newcastle Study', partly because of Jean's suspected aversion to alcohol and partly because he wanted to be in full possession of his faculties for whatever the fates might have in store.

At about quarter past ten he went to the loo, washed, and cleaned his teeth, then sat on the edge of the bed wondering what had happened to Jean.

At half past ten, after much thought, he opened the drawer marked 'Scottish and Newcastle Study' and took out a pack of six cans. He drank two quickly and, since he was on duty, slowed down over the next two. Still there was no sign of Jean. He finished the pack, undressed and went to bed, taking another pack of six cans over from the drawer to his bed, more or less as an afterthought.

Somewhat later in the night, he was aroused from a dream in which a girl, naked and loving, was climbing into bed beside him and taking hold of him quite unequivocally. He woke to find it true. He was seized by sudden remorse at being so drunk. In the dark he clung to her and sobbed into her shoulder, 'Oh, Jean. I'm sorry. Oh, Jean, Jean, Jean.'

'Wrong number,' said a familiar voice. Joan's.

'Bloody hell,' said Campbell. 'Sorry.'

They screwed anyway, and talked afterwards.

'I'm really sorry about that,' said Campbell. 'I was half expecting someone else.'

'Don't mention it,' said Joan. 'So was I. . . . At least I was until he rang up yesterday morning to say that after a lot of thought he'd decided to try to get someone else to do his ICU duty for him.'

'Bill?'

'Yes. Didn't you know? I thought everyone did.'

'I'd heard he had family problems.'

'I'm his family problem. Or I was until yesterday morning.'

'Oh. I'm sorry to hear that.'

'Don't be. We weren't particularly good for each other. He thought I understood him better than his wife. His main problem is his wife understands him all too well.'

'Poor Bill. You know I thought, after he asked me to swop, that it was funny he was still doing Saturdays on ICU.'

'He had special reasons.'

'I see. You.'

They both giggled, Campbell drunkenly, Joan tearfully, then they screwed again.

After that Joan excused herself on the grounds that the midnight break was supposed to be only half an hour. Campbell switched on the light and drank another can while she put on her uniform.

'How's the unit?'

'Quiet. Don't worry.'

'Goodnight.'

'Goodnight.'

Campbell found it difficult to get back to sleep, but managed after the second pack of cans was finished.

He woke next morning, feeling truly awful, with Joan sitting on his bed.

'Oh,' he said. 'It's you. Quiet night?'

'It was. For a while.'

'Anything happen?'

'One or two things. But you weren't worth waking. I tried.'

'Oh, Christ. . . . Perhaps not. What happened?'

'Three deaths. Two admissions. You've got quite a bit of paperwork to catch up on, Dr Campbell.' She produced the case notes and told him what to write. Even thus helped, he found it difficult. When they had finished she said, 'It might be best if you were up and ready to nip out fairly smartly when the day chap comes on. You're not looking your best.'

'All right. Thanks. Bye.'

'Bye. See you.'

'See you.'

Ill, and with the unreal, hollow feeling of having had a very narrow escape from medico-legal disaster, Campbell walked up through the Institute towards Creech's unit. He spent some minutes in the research fellows' toilet, trying to freshen up before going on to the ward.

Jean, calm and beautiful and efficient, was sitting at the desk in the duty room, with a heap of case folders, writing progress notes.

'Morning, Jean.'

'Morning, David.'

'Quiet night?'

'One of Creech's strokes died. An old lady.'

'Did she?'

'Mmm. Latish. Did you have a quiet night?'

'Fairly quiet.'

They looked at each other for a while. Campbell sat down and Jean said, 'You don't really look as if you've had a quiet night.'

'There were a few problems.'

'I came to see you, David.'

'Did you?'

'Very late. Just after midnight. . . . I wanted to talk to you. About Mrs Herron and . . . oh, about everything.'

'Oh?'

'I went down to ICU. . . . I knew the auxiliary in the kitchen there. . . . From before. So I got her to make us some Horlicks.'

'That was a kind thought.'

'But . . . when I went to take it in. . . . There were sort of . . . heavy-breathing noises.'

'Oh.'

'So I just went away again.'

She stood up and came quite close to Campbell, perhaps to smell his breath. 'Oh, David.'

'What?'

'Sometimes I worry about you.'

Campbell walked back across the park to his flat. The morning was calm and bright. In the distance the mad lady's troupe of dachshunds advanced on a broad front, fanning out from the arch of whales' jawbones. Rather nearer, at the place where the labourers had been working on the footpath, there was a lorry, looking lost so far from the road. Some more labourers were unloading picks, shovels and red warning lamps. As he passed, Campbell noticed turbid water welling up through the patch of fresh tarmac that marked the site of the previous week's excavation.

Rex Stout

'His stories of Nero Wolfe, that amiable epicure, always provide excitement, wit, unflagging interest and ingenuity.' *Books of Today*. 'If there is anyone in the civilised world who is not acquainted with Nero Wolfe, Mr Stout's large, overbearing investigator, here is the opportunity to plug a shameful gap . . .' *Evening Standard*. 'It is impossible for Rex Stout to be anything but supremely readable.' *Guardian*

THE GOLDEN SPIDERS 75p
DEATH OF A DUDE 50p
A FAMILY AFFAIR 70p
TOO MANY COOKS 75p
THE FATHER HUNT 75p
IF DEATH EVER SLEPT 80p
SOME BURIED CAESAR 80p

Fontana Paperbacks

Fontana Paperbacks

Fontana is a leading paperback publisher of fiction and non-fiction, with authors ranging from Alistair MacLean, Agatha Christie and Desmond Bagley to Solzhenitsyn and Pasternak, from Gerald Durrell and Joy Adamson to the famous Modern Masters series.

In addition to a wide-ranging collection of internationally popular writers of fiction, Fontana also has an outstanding reputation for history, natural history, military history, psychology, psychiatry, politics, economics, religion and the social sciences.

All Fontana books are available at your bookshop or newsagent; or can be ordered direct. Just fill in the form and list the titles you want.

FONTANA BOOKS, Cash Sales Department, G.P.O. Box 29, Douglas, Isle of Man, British Isles. Please send purchase price, plus 8p per book. Customers outside the U.K. send purchase price, plus 10p per book. Cheque, postal or money order. No currency.

NAME (Block letters)

ADDRESS

While every effort is made to keep prices low, it is sometimes necessary to increase prices on short notice. Fontana Books reserve the right to show new retail prices on covers which may differ from those previously advertised in the text or elsewhere.